CASSADY

JEFFERSON SUTTON

ST. MARTIN'S PRESS
NEW YORK

Library of Congress Cataloging in Publication Data

Sutton, Jefferson.
Cassady.

I. Title.
PZ4.S9668Cas   [PS3569.U89]   813'.5'4
                      79-16517
                 ISBN O-312-12343-4

For Andrew and Tyler

1

"JESUS, A TWENTY-FIVE thousand reward!" The young cop whistled softly, shifting his gaze from the newspaper to the elderly officer making out a report at a nearby desk. "How did Cassady get that kind of dough?"

"Inherited it." Larkin glanced up tiredly. "Some aunt in the East. Sam was the only relative."

"Plunking it down to try to find out who murdered his wife . . . fifteen years ago, it says."

"She was running a gift shop," Larkin offered. "A couple of punks walked in to hold her up and blasted her. She must have tried to put up a fight. Sam was just a rookie at the time, only married a couple of months. It's all there in the story."

"Any clues?"

"None worth a damn."

"Fifteen years . . ." The young cop whistled again. He'd been in grade school at the time. A long look back.

"Sam's never been worth a damn since."

"Oh? I heard he was pretty good."

"Better than most, I guess, but the fire's gone out of him. No ambition. When he first came on the force he was all piss and vinegar, a real goer—the kind of a guy you know is going right to the top." Larkin shook his head slowly. "Hell, he just made sergeant a few years ago."

"Sergeant's not bad," the young cop objected. It was a hurdle that lay, if he were lucky, several years in his future.

"Not bad at all," agreed Larkin, "but not good for a guy like Sam. He could have been right up there now if something in him hadn't died."

"Think the reward will do any good?"

"After fifteen years? Not a chance."

Three doors down from Larkin and the young cop, Sergeant Sam Cassady of the Traffic Division sat behind a scarred desk, contemplating the same story. A big man, rugged of face and graying at the temples, his eyes momentarily became unseeing as he strove to pull Nancy's image into his mind. Strange how it was fading. For years after her murder he had so easily resurrected her heart-shaped face, the deep blue eyes and corn-yellow hair . . . the way she gestured and walked and cocked her head enquiringly. Her light laugh, the softness of her voice, the things she'd whisper in the night—memories he'd treasured.

But then the fading had begun. Now she was receding farther and farther; her features, dimming, left only vague outlines in his memory. Even the large photograph of her on his dresser was becoming more and more like that of a stranger.

He shifted uneasily, guilty at the thought that the fading had begun the previous year, after he'd met Cindy. But a man couldn't cling to ghosts forever. A man was flesh and blood, had to live in the real world. Nancy would have understood that. Then why the guilt? Because he'd failed her? Because her killers still were free?

Such thoughts—and others far more discomfiting—had

2

come before, more frequently of late. Was he a prisoner of his own mind? Was that what drove him? Did he hope that finding the killers would free him . . . from Nancy? He rejected the last thought completely. No, he was a cop; there was a murder . . . a book to be closed. Wasn't that what justice was all about?

Cassady glanced back at the story without really seeing it. Since her murder he'd spent long off-duty hours trying to find some trace of the killers. He'd had but three slim leads: an eyewitness report of two slender youths—both of medium height with overly-long hair—fleeing the scene; death bullets fired from a .25-caliber automatic; an unusual gold wristwatch set in diamonds—his wedding present to her.

During those fifteen years he'd made it a point to scrutinize the record of every man arrested for armed robbery, to no avail. He'd become a familiar figure in the Stats Office, which maintained a file of punch cards on all known criminals within the department's jurisdiction. And in Records and Information, where all criminal "packages" were filed. He'd kept escalating their ages with the passing years; now they'd probably be in their middle thirties. Still together? Quite unlikely. But they could be fat, thin, bald, nattily-attired or in rough work clothes; masked by the anonymity of family or job; they could be in the pen or in some distant city . . . or under headstones. Yet he knew that murder was seldom committed in a vacuum. Someone, somewhere, would know the killers' names, and if they still lived and where. His sole hope was that the reward might induce someone with the guilty knowledge to speak. A slim hope, he knew, but a hope. Oh, he'd get plenty of calls; he had no doubt of that. Kooks and con artists and the frankly curious or sympathetic would be ringing his number like mad. Yet, among those calls . . . .

He stared woodenly at the story.

After a while he glanced at his watch, rose and went to

3

the parking lot. Cutting toward the freeway, his thoughts were of Cindy O'Neal. They had hit it off together right from the start. Strange, too, because she was almost the opposite of Nancy. Slender, dark-haired and dark-eyed, she stood a good four inches taller. Nancy had been quiet, introspective; Cindy was blunt and extroverted. A widow for four years, she had eight-year-old twin boys that Cassady was coming more and more to think of as the sons he'd never had. Not that Cindy was dangling the marriage hook—she was much too forthright for that—but the expectation was there. He sensed it in her quiet demeanor when, after their love-making, she lay with the bedside lamp splashing its light across her body. At such times he felt small stabs of guilt. But when this was over, when Nancy's killers were brought to justice . . . He knew she understood that.

It was part of her waiting.

Cassady swung off the freeway onto a quiet tree-lined street and parked in front of an old two-story apartment house. Getting out, he rustled in his pocket for the key and started toward the stairs. He opened the door to the sound of his phone.

"First kook," he told himself.

The name on the frosted glass door read SOUTHWEST INVESTMENT ENTERPRISES. Beyond it, a slender brunette secretary with sultry almond-shaped eyes sat at an electric typewriter. The carpeting, a deep shag, held the hue of green sea water. The walnut-paneled walls were adorned with water colors of Mexican scapes, and heavy brocaded drapes blanked the view of the smoggy city from the wide windows. The room was quiet, anonymous in the swirl of the twenty-story Crossman Building in which it was located.

4

Behind the secretary, the frosted pane of a second door bore the name *Angelo Geraci*, and below it, the title *President*.

Inside, Geraci sat at a large walnut desk, his jowly face, deeply tanned from the radiation of sunlamps, introspective. At the moment, reading about the reward, his mind had retreated fifteen years into the past.

The ghosts leaped.

He could see the woman—a slender young blonde—a hand thrown to her mouth, screaming as he'd shot her. All for a lousy thirty-eight bucks. That and a diamond-studded wristwatch too hot to handle.

Skousen had argued about that. If they had pawned the watch, like Skousen had wanted, they would have been picked up before the week was out. He'd settled that by grinding it into the pavement with the flat of his heel. Skousen had been sore as hell. But he'd learned a lesson, Geraci reflected—never do business with a damn fool. He'd cut loose from Skousen that same night. He rubbed his jaw. The crime had been all but forgotten in the passage of time. How long? Fifteen years. Now, suddenly, there was a twenty-five-thousand-dollar reward.

Sam Cassady, a sergeant in the Traffic Division. Where would a traffic cop get twenty-five grand? He could understand it if he were in vice or narcotics, but traffic? More to the point, what did he expect to find after fifteen years? Nothing, and in that respect his twenty-five big ones were safe. Publicity—that was what they all wanted. A big fucking splash bought at no risk. Still . . .

He felt uneasy. Cassady didn't sound like a kook . . . a guy looking for a spread. Geraci fancied he knew men, their weaknesses and strengths, and he had a disquieting feeling about this one, a feeling reinforced by the photograph that accompanied the story. A big, rugged-looking bastard, strong jaw, dark hair graying at the temples, wide-spread eyes that held an implacable look. No kook. And no patsy.

5

But why, after fifteen years? Had he picked up a whisper? No, that wasn't possible. Unless . . .

Skousen . . . Frank Skousen. He hadn't thought of him in years—not since Skousen had drifted away, a goddamned monkey riding his back. Geraci racked his memory. Last he'd heard, Skousen had been on the pavement, begging and stealing to support his habit. He could be down there somewhere now, on East Fifth, or living in one of the ten thousand warrens that dotted the side streets. Could he have bragged to someone, trying to build up his shredded ego? A babe, maybe—some down-at-the-heels hooker. Christ, the things a guy told in bed.

The reward! If Skousen saw that . . . The thought, unnerving, brought a moment of panic. But Skousen couldn't angle for that without putting his own head in the noose. Or could he? What if he tried to collect through a third party—sell just one name? *Angelo Geraci*. Would Frankie have the guts for that? Money, envy, vengeance . . . a guy in the gutter might try anything. Or if he'd already blabbed to someone . . .

Geraci swore softly. Skousen might or might not be alive, might or might not have blabbed; but if alive, he could be dangerous. And if alive, he could be found and made to talk. And if he talked . . . Geraci felt the soft thrust of fear. He should have taken care of the bastard years ago. Well, it wasn't too late—a piece of meat he could toss to Pinto. Pinto would love that.

He reached for the phone, hesitated. But then Pinto would know; he'd put that one together fast. Would that be any worse than a hundred other things Pinto knew? If he couldn't trust Pinto, who could he trust?

Geraci began to dial.

"Did you read about that cop offering twenty-five thousand for information on his wife's murder?" asked Bennie the Needle. "That bastard must really be on the take."

"What are you talking about?" Shaking, as with fever and chills, Frank Skousen watched Bennie empty a thin paper of white powder into the cooker and add a few drops of water, measuring the amount by eye.

"Some cop trying to find out who killed his wife," explained Bennie. "A guy named Cassady; it's on the front page."

"Cassady did you say?" Skousen jerked upright in the chair, feeling a hollow thump in his chest.

"What's wrong?" Bennie eyed him curiously.

"Christ, that was a long time ago." Skousen wet his lips nervously. "Fifteen . . . fifteen years."

"How do you know?"

"Know?" Skousen jerked back his attention, tight with fright. "I heard some guy talking about it . . . over in the pool hall," he added lamely.

"Oh?" Bennie's eyes grew speculative. "Who?"

"How should I know," Skousen asked sullenly. "Just some guy poppin' off. Hurry with that damned fix, will ya? I'm comin' apart."

"This stuff's gettin' hard to come by since the crackdown."

"You're gettin' paid, ain'tcha?"

"Yeah, sure." Bennie moved the cooker over the flame. "They're burnin' the goddamned poppy fields down in Mexico. Helicopters yet."

"Christ, hurry."

"Gotta cook it right." As the solution began to boil, Bennie sucked it up into a dropper through a small cotton filter. Skousen twisted a piece of rubber tubing around his arm to make the vein on the inside of his left elbow stand out. Bennie attached a hypodermic needle to the dropper and eyed the scarred tissue critically. "Ya ought to start hittin' the ankle," he advised.

"Jesus, get to it."

7

Bennie prodded with the needle. Sliding it under the skin, he maneuvered until he found a vein. Letting the blood rise in the dropper to mix with the dissolved heroin, he shot the entire solution back into the bloodstream.

"Ahhh . . ." Skousen experienced a small orgasm in his central nervous system as the tension left his body, replaced by a curious serenity. His dark eyes seemed to stare deeply into a distant and quiet void.

Bennie dipped the needle into a jar of alcohol, filled the syringe and squirted the fluid back into the jar. Replacing the needle and dropper in the kit, he looked at Skousen. "This stuff's gettin' hard to come by, Frankie. The price is really goin' to jump."

"Yeah, sure," he answered dreamily. In the euphoria brought on by the white powder, he could care less about Bennie's troubles. Besides, they could burn Mexico from border to border and the stuff would still flow in; the profit margin guaranteed that.

"That story just hit the papers."

"Story?"

"The cop offering the twenty-five G's."

"Screw Cassady," Skousen said placidly. He picked up his jacket and turned toward the door.

Bennie listened to the receding footsteps on the wooden stairs. Skousen's reaction to the cop's name had been too startled. Nor had Bennie missed the sudden fear in Skousen's eyes. His imagination? He didn't think so. Yet what could a bum like Skousen possibly know about the crime? Twenty-five thousand. Bennie whistled softly. A man could go a long way on that kind of bread.

Sprawled on a dirty bed in his shabby room, Skousen enjoyed the images that sailed like small golden ships through his mind. The drug, after the first wave of euphoria had passed, always left him with the pleasant sensation of mind and body being divorced from the reality of his surroundings. The noise of the traffic just below his window sounded more like the low murmur of distant tides, and in place of the grimy walls and tattered curtains, a golden sea surrounded him. He would enjoy the splendid isolation until the stabbing hunger pangs again thrust into his consciousness and his body screamed with need, but even that seemed to lie far away in time.

Cassady offering twenty-five big ones . . . The idea struck him as humorous and he giggled. Twenty-five thousand was a hell of a lot to pay for a dead woman . . . how many years? Fifteen. Jesus, Dandy had really fixed her.

Detachedly, as if reviewing some half-forgotten film, he pulled the fragments together in his mind. *The chick's frightened face . . . a hand to her mouth . . . the beginning of a scream . . . the flat bark of the .25 automatic that looked small even in Dandy's slender hand*—the pictures swirled in slow motion, gradually filling in the gaps like fog creeping in along a waterfront street. How much had they got? Thirty-eight bucks. Yeah, and a watch. He remembered the watch—a small thing with diamonds encircling the face. He'd snatched it from her wrist, then afterward Dandy had decided it was too hot to pawn and had crushed it with his shoe. Maybe he was right. Man, a guy could stumble on something like that and wind up on hot street. He would never have risked the robbery in the first place if it hadn't been for Dandy.

"Nothing to it," Dandy had told him, "when they see that rod, they give." The small gift shop had been Dandy's idea, too. "Those guys in liquor stores always have a gun handy," he'd explained. "Pick a place where they have a chick working and you've got it made." His philosophy was that you could knock over four or five such small shops and come out with as much as you'd get at a going liquor store with none of the attendant risks.

9

Only it hadn't worked that way. The woman had started to scream and Dandy's small automatic had barked. A cop's wife, at that. Despite his lassitude Skousen shivered at the memory. Man, he'd jumped at his own shadow for six months afterward. But that hadn't stopped Dandy.

Recollection brought a faint bitterness mixed with regret. If he'd stuck with Dandy he'd be somebody now. Tailored suits and fat cigars and big cars . . . broads with class instead of a dog who had to turn tricks on East Fifth to make the price of a fix.

Screw it, he thought languidly, Dandy could have his soft living. Only he wasn't Dandy anymore; he was Angelo Geraci, big-shot president of Southwest Investment Enterprises. Yeah, he knew all about that business. Manny had told him once when he was drunk, and since then he'd heard a lot more. The Syndicate, that's what. Jesus, put a man in a swank office and give it a fancy name and everyone pretended he was someone else. Like being born again.

He felt the envy pressing back. Geraci at the race track . . . on his yacht at Balboa . . . in the financial section. Only he knew what lay behind the pictures. Dandy still had his paws on the prostitution and porn and gambling all over town. And drugs—Geraci was probably the bastard pushing up the price. That would be Dandy, all right. Man, he even squeezed a few bucks out of Lois for her lousy humpin' on East Fifth.

"Fuck Dandy," he thought. Closing his eyes, he drifted off to sleep.

2

"HEY, IT'S UNCLE SAM," cried Eddie.

"Uncle Sam," his twin brother shouted. Both boys charged toward the curb as the squad car drew up. Cassady clambered out.

"Very patriotic," he observed. It was an old gag but they all laughed. "Why aren't you in school?"

"We got ten minutes yet," Eddie explained.

"What's in the car?" Chuck peered in through a window.

"A present for your mother." Cassady blushed and brought out a long box.

"Flowers?" Eddie looked innocent.

"None of your business, young man." Cassady made a production of looking at his watch. "You don't want to be late."

"We can get there in two minutes," Chuck said disdainfully.

Eddie grinned. "I think Uncle Sam wants us to go now."

"Run along," urged Cassady. He tucked the long box under his arm and turned toward the porch. Cindy met him at the door.

11

"You remembered," she exclaimed.

"Roses for your twenty-fifth birthday." He extended the box.

"Add ten," she said primly, "but thank you. Come in?"

"Only a moment." He followed her into the small front room and watched her open the box.

"They're beautiful!" She clasped the red roses to her.

"I was going to ask you out tonight . . . celebrate, but I won't be able to make it," he apologized.

"The reward?"

"I'm getting a flood of calls."

"Any that might be helpful?"

"Mostly con artists," he admitted. "They offer a few details that were in the newspapers at the time as proof they have inside information; just trying to squeeze out a few thousand. I imagine a lot of guys are down at the library going through the old files."

"What dreadful people."

"The world's full of them."

"Would anyone know . . . after all this time?"

"Someone knows, Cindy."

"I hope so. For your sake, I hope so." She laid the flowers back in the box. "Coffee?"

"No time." He looked wistfully at her dark, slender face before he kissed her, holding her tight.

Finally she pushed him back. "You'd better leave or we'll both be late. Very late, Mr. Cassady."

"I'd love that." He grinned and kissed her again before taking his departure.

Driving along the boulevard, he wondered if he were being foolish. He could start his new life now; there was nothing to stop him. A new home . . . Cindy and the boys. A small dream in a big world, but it was all he wanted. It would be good to come home to her every night . . . wake with her every morning. She could quit pounding the typewriter, make a real home for the kids. Cindy and Chuck and Eddie—a tailor-made family. He couldn't ask for more. Yet, would the unrest remain? On a slow burner, maybe, but he knew it would persist; he'd gone on too long to quit now. At least he had to let the reward ride until he knew it was hopeless.

Hopeless? He found himself denying it. There must be ten thousand informers in town . . . and guys with grudges. *Someone knew*! Christ, those words hung like a millstone around his neck—drove him on and on and on. But someone did know . . . and would talk. Besides, the book was never closed on murder. Not till the case was solved. Not till then would he be free of the spur that drove him. He'd always known that. Since meeting Cindy, the need had become imperative. If the reward didn't do it . . .

His radio crackled to life. He reluctantly pushed aside his thoughts and acknowledged. A bad accident at the intersection of Fern and Evert. He tromped on the gas pedal, turned on the siren.

Another bloody day on the streets had begun.

Skousen woke, the room gray in the light of morning. Stale musty odors assailed his nostrils and from beyond the window came the harsh sounds of traffic. A flushing toilet rattled pipes in the wall.

He struggled to a sitting position at the edge of the bed. The bra and skirt draped over the straight-back chair and the half-open dresser drawer were exactly the same as when he'd come home. The bitch had stayed away all night again. His resentment was masked by the sick, gnawing hunger he felt in the pit of his stomach. Despite the early coolness, his body felt sweaty. God, he needed a fix.

He started to reach for his clothes before he remembered he was broke. Where in Christ was Lois? Turned an all-night trick, now was out somewhere blowing it in. Just like a goddamned woman. He was pulling on his socks when he heard her footsteps on the stairs. He looked up resentfully as she came into the room. "Where the hell have you been?"

"What do you care?" she snapped. She slipped off her worn jacket and went to the mirror, fingering the pale blemishes on her skin. The reflection showed a narrow face, flesh taut over high cheekbones, thin lips, dark eyes that dwelt in a wasteland of purple hollows. She looked a solid forty but he knew her to be a good dozen years younger. From time to time she shot furtive glances at him while completing her inspection.

Skousen felt the growing sickness, the crumbling of his nerves. "Got any money?" He hated the whining tone of his voice.

"It's always money." She swung around. "Why don't you get a job?"

"Please, I need a fix."

"You always need a fix. Why don't you get your own kit? You know that bastard Bennie overcharges us; besides, he cuts it to the bone."

"How long would I last with my own kit? I can't walk down the street without getting frisked. Those damned narcs watch every step I take."

"That's your imagination. Just because you've been picked up a few times . . ."

"Please . . ."

"Do like I do, earn it."

"I know how you cash in," he said bitterly.

"I'm getting my fill of Bennie."

"Until you need a fix. That's where you were all night, isn't it?"

"So what?" Her eyes picked up in sudden interest. "He was really curious about you."

"Me? Why?" Fear knotted his stomach.

"He wanted to know if you ever talked about a cop named Cassady."

14

"Cassady?" He licked his lips, trying to conceal a tremor. "What did you tell him?"

"Nothing, why should I?" She stepped closer. "What about Cassady?"

"Well, nothing."

"You know something!"

"It wasn't anything, honest."

"No?"

"Christ, give me some dough. I need a fix."

"Not till you tell me about Cassady."

"The cop was offering a reward, that was all. Something to do with the murder of his wife."

"Twenty-five thousand, Bennie said."

"You talked with him about it," he accused.

"He just mentioned it."

"I'll bet."

"What do you know about it?"

"Just something I heard . . . at the pool hall."

"What?"

"Christ, Lois . . ."

"Do you want that fix or don'tcha?"

"You don't know what you're askin'," he moaned. "Think I want to wind up in an alley with my throat cut?"

"Of course not." She sat on the bed beside him and patted his bony knee. "Twenty-five thousand is a lot of money," she coaxed.

"Stop it, I tell you. It's a cut throat, nothin' else."

"You'd never have to depend on Bennie again."

"Shut up, damn you!"

"You need a fix, Frankie."

"Damned right I do, that's what I've been telling you."

"It's just that I hate to see Bennie get that twenty-five thousand."

"What he'll get is a knife in an alley!"

"Oh, he wouldn't take a chance; he'd use a go-between."

"Yeah, if he knew."

"You know, Frankie. You could do the same . . . use a go-between."

"Nix, I told you that."

"Maybe me."

"You?" He watched her, sensing she had knowledge and plans that lay just beyond the border of his understanding. A cold shiver ran through his body.

"Maybe I could make a deal without using your name, Frankie. Ever think of that?"

"With that goddamned cop?"

"Who else?"

"Yeah, sure, and you'd have to go to court to testify. How long d'ya think you'd last? Those guys are rough. Jesus, you should know; you've been paying them long enough."

"The Syndicate," she said slowly, "you're talking about the Syndicate." When he didn't answer, she continued, "He might pay for that information."

"What information?"

"That the Syndicate was involved, but I'd have to know enough about it to hook him."

"Know what he'd do? He'd bleed you for everything you know, then run you in."

"I don't know anything yet."

"Jesus, Lois . . ."

"Tell me what you know—what Cassady would pay to know."

"I don't know nothin', I tell you."

"You know something."

"I know I need a fix!"

"Sure, Frankie."

"Where's the dough?" She rose and walked to the dresser and picked up her purse. He eyed it greedily. She opened it, glanced inside and shut it again. "Give me the dough!" His mouth felt cottony.

"Tell me," she said stonily.

"It was nothin'."

She started toward the door.

"Wait," he pleaded. She turned slowly, watching him.

He licked his lips. "There was a watch . . . something about a watch."

"What about the watch?"

"One of the guys took it from her."

"You?"

"God, no!" he exploded. Christ, why had he told her? Fear suffused his face.

"What about the watch?"

"It was diamond-studded. At least I heard it was."

"From who?"

"A guy at the pool hall . . . just poppin' off."

"Of course, Frankie."

"That's all I know," he said sullenly.

"You really need a fix, don'tcha?" She opened her purse again and fumbled inside before bringing out some wrinkled bills. "Get yourself some breakfast," she advised.

"Yeah, sure." He dressed hurriedly, conscious of the growing distress in his body. Now that he had the money the need was more imperative than ever. The nausea had seeped into bone and muscle and flesh alike so that every single cell seemed to scream in agony. God, if he hadn't gotten the money . . .

Lois watched him, wetting her lips as if to underscore her thoughts. He kept his eyes averted from her, fearful at what she might say. A goddamned whore; he'd never trusted any of them. At the door he turned back hesitantly. "You won't say anything, will you?"

"About what?" she mocked.

"What I told you."

"Of course not, Frankie." Her smile was brittle.

Skousen entered a dim hallway, climbed the worn stairs

to the second floor and rapped on a door. When he heard no sound of movement inside he rapped louder. The answering silence brought a quick, panicky feeling.

Bennie wasn't in! His hands shook violently. Jesus, it couldn't be true; Bennie was always in. Maybe he went out for breakfast. He grasped at the hope. If so, he wouldn't be gone long. Couldn't be.

He retreated slowly down the stairs, crossed the street and entered Dave's Cafe, taking a stool by the window so he could watch the entrance to Bennie's apartment. Although he hadn't eaten since the previous afternoon, his hunger was lost in a welling sickness. Ordering coffee, he stared through the dirty glass.

A rail-thin man named Brady came in and sat a few stools away. He, too, ordered coffee, enclosing the cup in his trembling hands. Brady was on speed. Skousen watched him, wondering if he looked as shaky and sick, then knew he did and turned back to watch the street. God, why didn't Bennie hurry?

His eyes fell on Flash, a slender Chicano garbed in a bright yellow sports jacket and tan slacks that held a knife-edge crease. Flash was a Murphy man, yeah, and a take-off artist, who obtained money from panicky junkies on the promise of making a score. Instead, he'd take off with the money, leaving his victims in more dire straits than ever. He'd worked that angle a few times himself before shacking up with Lois, finding it easier and safer to obtain money from her.

A glimpse of a figure at the far end of the block brought him upright before other pedestrians obscured his view. But it was Bennie, had to be; there was no mistaking that thin face atop the lumpy, ungainly body. Bennie always held his head as if sniffing the breeze with his long, twitchy nose. There! He breathed easier as Bennie came into view again. He wore his usual rumpled blue suit and a dirty white shirt open at the collar.

18

Skousen shoved his cup aside and hurried across the street, following him up the stairs. Bennie heard his footsteps and whirled back, visibly relieved when he saw who it was. "Don't scare me that way," he snapped.

"I've been waiting."

"So?" Bennie proceeded to his door, opened it and Skousen followed him into the shabby room. Bennie went to the window and peered out between the soiled curtains before turning back. "If you've come for a fix you're out of luck."

"Out of luck?" Skousen repeated numbly. He felt his stomach roil.

"I told you that stuff was hard to get."

"You've got some," Skousen whined, "you always have."

Bennie shook his head. "Not till later."

"God, I can't wait! I'm comin' apart!"

"Try me around noon."

"That's nearly three hours," he cried.

"Can't be helped, Frankie. Maybe you can score somewhere else." Bennie's tone clearly said the attempt would be futile. Listening to Skousen's pleading, Bennie gauged the desperation in his eyes.

Skousen swung toward the bathroom, where Bennie usually kept his kit. The son of a bitch was holding out; he knew it. He had the wild urge to assault him but knew Bennie could crush him like a bug. "Please," he begged.

"Noon, I said, and the price is up . . . another five."

"I've got it," he said eagerly.

"Lois is really humpin', eh?" Bennie waved him imperiously from the room and shut the door behind him. Wretched, Skousen returned to the cafe, got another cup of coffee and resumed his vigil at the window. If Bennie wasn't carrying, who would be? His clothes damp with sweat and his heart pounding wildly, he felt the nausea rolling through him in great crashing waves.

He looked at the clock above the counter: 9:35. A seeming eternity later it read 10:15. God, noon . . . how long till noon? He'd never make it. Never, never . . . He was going to die right here on the goddamned stool. He tore his eyes from the clock. Better not watch it.

Sight of a thin man in gray turning in at the entrance to Bennie's apartment brought a flare of hope. Maybe Bennie was having the stuff delivered! He forced himself to keep from dashing across the street, knowing how sore Bennie would be if he busted in during a transaction. He looked at the clock: nearly 11:30. That was it, he told himself fervently.

Several minutes later the thin man in gray emerged and turned back the way he had come. Skousen ran from the cafe and dashed across the street, unmindful of the din of horns. A truck swerved to avoid hitting him and the driver swore angrily. Skousen scarcely heard him.

At the top of the stairs he knocked impatiently at Bennie's door. The wait seemed interminable before it opened. Before he could speak, Bennie said, "Not yet. Not till around two."

"The Man came," Skousen cried. "I saw him."

Bennie shook his head. "Some guy trying to score, Frankie. His regular source got busted. Like I said, the lid's on."

"If you haven't got it by now, how do you know you'll have it by two?"

"You tryin' to make trouble?"

"No, but . . ."

"Two o'clock," snapped Bennie. He stepped back and slammed the door.

Skousen scarcely knew how he got back to the cafe. Waiting by the window, he began to shake uncontrollably and jerked his hands from the cup to keep from spilling the remains of his cold coffee. The skinny gray-haired man behind the counter eyed him sympathetically. Having taken the cure several times, he knew exactly what Skousen was going through.

After what seemed hours Skousen looked back at the

clock; the big hand had scarcely moved. Goddamn Bennie, he had to find another place to score. He was a damned fool to give his dough to a prick like that. But maybe the lid was on! If it was, how did Bennie expect to get the stuff at two? Or was he holding out to jack the price still higher?

He sensed someone sliding onto the stool alongside him and turned, recognizing Flash.

"Man, you look hung over," the Chicano said.

"God, I need a fix." Skousen eyed him desperately. "That goddamned Bennie says the town's drying up."

"Bennie said that?" Flash appeared surprised. "Hell, man, I've got a solid connection."

"You have?"

"Good stuff. None of that garbage that Bennie peddles. Mine is real dynamite."

"Honest to God?" Skousen watched him uncertainly, knowing his reputation.

"I've got it but it might be a little stiff for your league. None of that twenty-buck stuff."

"How much?" Skousen felt his doubts dissolve in the bright prospect dangling before his eyes.

"Twenty-five . . . that's the basement."

"I've only got twenty," he whined.

Flash appeared to consider it. "Tell you what," he said finally, "I'll trust you for the other five."

"You'll get it tomorrow," Skousen said eagerly. When he brought out the crumpled bills Flash plucked them from his hand.

"Wait here," he instructed. Skousen watched him vanish through the doorway, sick with the almost certain knowledge that he'd been taken. Yet what choice did he have? Maybe Flash would score for him. He caught the skinny waiter's eyes, saw him shake his head slowly in negation.

At a few minutes before two, Skousen lurched up from his stool and teetered across the street, the bitterness of having been conned erased by the screaming need within

21

him. Bennie opened the door with a smile that was more promising.

"You've got it?" Skousen blurted. Bennie nodded, regarding Skousen's unkempt figure speculatively as he closed the door behind him.

"But things are damned tough, Frankie. Like I said, the price has jumped to twenty-five bucks."

"Twenty-five?" Skousen stared at him, then said quickly, "You'll get it."

"Now," said Bennie.

"Jesus, I haven't got it. That damned Flash—you know him!—took me for it while I was waiting. But I'll bring it right back, honest. Lois is turning a trick right now."

"Don't kid me, Frankie. Who'd pay that much for her fanny?"

"Honest, she started early."

"No credit, I don't deal that way."

"You know I'm good for it," Skousen whined.

"No dice."

"But Lois . . ."

"If she's got a roomful lined up it won't take long—not the way she operates."

"I can't wait, Bennie, I can't!"

"That's your problem, Frankie."

"Please," he begged.

"Well . . ." Bennie appeared indecisive.

"Please," he repeated.

"Maybe, just this once . . ." Bennie went to the bathroom and returned with the kit. Unzipping it, he drew out the spoon with the bent handle that served as the cooker, next brought out a syringe and a small flat paper containing the white powder. Skousen watched him avidly. His movements slow and deliberate, Bennie lit the stub of a candle and placed it on the table alongside him before he eyed Skousen again.

"Cook it," Skousen urged, "I can't wait."

Bennie shook his head. "I've been thinking."

"About what?" Skousen tried to control his jitters. His nerves twitched and jumped, his body was one massive ache and sweat coursed down his bony frame. Damn Bennie, why was he waiting? He'd promised to pay, hadn't he?

"That cop Cassady, who offered the twenty-five big ones." Bennie's eyes grew cold. "You know about it."

"Only what I heard."

"What was that?"

"Some guy talkin', like I told you. I hardly listened."

"That's your tough shit, Frankie." Bennie snuffed out the candle and replaced the syringe and cooker in the kit.

"What are you doing?" Alarm flooded Skousen's face.

"No money, no sale, Frankie."

"You've gotta, please. I'm sick, Bennie, I can't stand it."

"Try somewhere else."

"I'm broke, I told you that. That damned Flash took me. Jesus, give me a break." Tears stung his eyes.

"Then tell me about Cassady."

"I would if I could."

"You were in it, weren't you? You and someone else."

"That's a lie," he screamed.

"Is it, Frankie?"

"Cook it, please."

"You don't trust me, do you, Frankie?"

"Sure I do; you're my friend, Bennie."

"You don't trust me enough to tell me."

"Tell you what?"

"The names Cassady wants."

"Jesus, I don't know. That's the truth, Bennie."

"Is it?" Bennie zipped the bag closed.

"I'm not lying," Skousen sobbed.

Bennie peered at him. "I study people, Frankie. Did you know that? I can tell when a man's lying."

"Why would I lie to you?" he groaned.

"Because you're scared Cassady will learn you were in on it." Bennie pursed his lips thoughtfully. "What do you think the other guy will do when he hears about the reward? He'll figure some way of selling you, Frankie."

"He couldn't," exclaimed Skousen.

"Why not?"

"He'd be cutting his own throat."

"So I was right." Bennie nodded, satisfied that his guess had paid off. He opened the kit again. Lighting the candle, he poured the white powder into the spoon and measured in the water. Skousen watched him, scarcely daring to breathe. Bennie moved the cooker toward the flame, hesitated.

"Cook it," gasped Skousen. He wound the flexed tubing around his arm to raise the vein.

"No." Bennie shook his head.

"For God's sake, Bennie."

"The other name!"

"Please, he'd cut my throat!"

"This is my last jolt, Frankie. I'm going to dump it."

"Don't do that," he screamed.

"Then give me the fucking name!"

Skousen stared at him, gripped in an awful sickness. It was as if every cell in his body had sensed the presence of the drug, and was screaming for its share. Bennie's thin face above the candle flame held a waiting expression. Skousen wanted to throw himself at Bennie's feet and beg him but he knew it would do no good. His body jerked convulsively.

"Geraci," he whispered hoarsely.

"Angelo Geraci?" Bennie's head snapped up. Skousen nodded numbly. "Jesus H. Christ," Bennie whispered.

His eyes searched Skousen's face for a long moment before he moved the cooker over the flame.

"We can work it with no risk on a fifty-fifty split," said Bennie.

"Why should I split?" Lois eyed him across the shabby room. The thin face with its close-set dark eyes and needle nose held an assurance that perturbed her. Was he trying to grab the whole reward for himself? If so, why had he propositioned her?

"You can't work it alone," he counseled.

"What makes you think I'm after the reward?"

"Because I know you, Lois. You wouldn't be damned fool enough to let that one get by you."

She waited.

"You still can't work it alone," he repeated.

"Why not?"

"You'd have to know the name of the guy who was in on it with Frankie—or did he tell you?"

"Who said Frankie was in on it?" she demanded.

"He told me. He was hungry for a fix."

"You're a goddamned bastard."

"Sure, but that doesn't change things; you still can't swing it alone."

"You hope. Besides, I don't know the name."

"You know something else . . . something that makes you think you can collect. A clue maybe."

"That's my business."

"That's it, a clue, something that will convince the cop, but the other name's the thing that will swing the deal." When she didn't respond, he continued, "Suppose someone tipped the other fellow that you were squealing to Cassady?"

"I always said you were a no-good son of a bitch," she flared.

"Hear who's talking."

"What if I passed the word *you* were a stoolie?"

"To who? I thought you didn't know the guy's name."

She tossed her head. "Frankie will tell me."

"Try to work it by yourself and you won't last long. That guy will carve off those big hanging tits."

"Some Syndicate punk." Lois nervously crushed her cigarette in a dirty ashtray. "Frankie practically said as much but that doesn't scare me. A punk's a punk."

"Would you like to try it for size?" When her eyes came up, waiting, he said, "Angelo Geraci."

"I don't believe it!" She sprang from her chair. "You're trying to scare me."

"You'd better believe it." He eyed her contentedly. "You might spring the name on Frankie—watch his reaction. He'll crap his pants, baby."

She sat again, rustling in her purse for another cigarette. He watched her light it, then said, "You couldn't run fast enough or far enough. He'd shove a hot pipe up you, slice you to ribbons. However, if we work together . . ."

She wet her lips nervously. "Count me out. I don't want any part of that bastard."

"You know the name; that makes you part of it." He added soothingly, "But we don't have to involve Geraci. Like I said, it's plenty safe. We only need one name."

"Frankie?" she whispered.

"What's that son of a bitch ever done for you besides cash in on your fanny?"

"He's all right."

"You like mothering the slob, eh?"

"Why can't we just pick a name out of the hat? If he knows I know, why wouldn't he buy that . . . a phony name?"

"Plenty of con artists are probably trying that right now." He shook his head. "You gotta give him something that'll add up to a conviction."

"You mean go to court? God, never!" She puffed her cigarette nervously.

"If the cops grab Frankie they'll make him spill his guts; that'll take you off the hook. Look at what you could do with twelve-five," he urged. "You could set yourself up in a nice swank apartment, really live it up. It's time you tied into a permanent daddy, baby. You haven't many good years left."

"Have you?"

"That's why I'm dealing you in. I want the dough now."

"Besides which you can't collect without me," she snapped.

"No?" He smiled. "I could always get another hooker, cut her in, give her Frankie's name. Plenty of broads would snap at that bait."

She fussed with her bag before looking back at him. "Would he pay that much for one name?"

"If your clue's good enough."

"It is."

He leaned back, suddenly relaxed. "Now here's how we'll work it . . ."

3

CASSADY WAS SETTLING DOWN with a drink when the phone rang—the fifth call in the short time since he'd arrived home. Another kook, he thought. He set the glass on a coffee table and lifted the receiver.

"Mr. Cassady?" The female voice held a nervous, throaty sound. He acknowledged, placing his caller around thirty and—for some reason unknown to him—he had a mental image of her as tall, on the dark side. In the past he'd found such snap impressions reasonably accurate.

"About the reward," she said hesitantly. "I have information."

"What kind?"

"A name, but I'm not going to just tell you."

"I'm home for the night," he encouraged. He gave his address and asked, "Where are you calling from?"

"Why?" She sounded defiant.

"I thought you might need information on how to get here," he explained.

"I can find it." A click came through the receiver and the line went dead. He slowly replaced the instrument. Since the story had appeared in the press dozens of people of both sexes had called. Most had been trying to peddle the few facts they'd scraped up, or had been fishing for information which undoubtedly they'd hoped to use later to convince him they had inside information. Some of the female callers had been under the impression that a lonely cop with twenty-five thousand to spare might be in need of solace. Others were simply crank calls or people harboring grudges. One irate wife had named her husband. He'd quickly dispensed with those.

This caller was different; he felt that instinctively. A name! She hadn't beat around the bush about that. He let a faint hope glow for a moment before suppressing it; he'd seen too many hopes quashed to let another flower without something substantial to go on.

He changed into a pair of tan slacks, a brown sport shirt and moccasins that he thought made him look less like a cop, then he moved his old Ford in front of the building. Afterward he placed his chair by a window that gave him a clear view of the street below.

Several minutes later a taxi cruised slowly toward him and pulled up in front of the entrance. A dark-haired woman emerged. Her age and height appeared about as he'd guessed, but she was hippier than he'd supposed. After paying the driver, she scanned the windows briefly before entering the building.

Her knock was hesitant.

His first impression upon opening the door was of unkemptness—a blue blouse and tan skirt badly wrinkled and soiled, scuffed white sandals over bare feet, hair a tangled mess. Her thin face held a hard, ravaged look. He stepped back. "Come in, please." She walked past him without answering. "Care for some coffee?"

She turned to face him, veiled fright in her eyes. "I won't be long."

"Have a seat." He gestured toward a chair. She jerked

her head in a nod, rustled in her purse for a cigarette and sat gingerly, as if prepared to flee.

Cassady tabbed her as a hooker from the wrong side of the tracks. It was all there—the grubby clothes, the harshness in her face, eyes that had seen it all. Lighting the cigarette, she inhaled deeply before asking, "Is the reward for real?"

"If the information is valid, yes." He sat opposite her.

"You mean true? It's true all right, but I won't testify—nothing like that."

"What kind of information?"

She watched him, her eyes calculating. "A name, I told you that."

"Just one?"

She jerked her head in a nod.

"You could give me any name," he suggested. "How can you prove what you say?"

"There was a watch—a small gold watch set in diamonds."

Cassady suppressed a sharp intake of breath. The watch had never been mentioned in the news. The hope had been that the killers would pawn it, thus giving another trace of them. Such had not happened. Now, again . . . the watch! Cassady had the impending feeling of standing at the border of some vast revelation. Nothing of that showed on his face.

"You might still give me a phoney name," he said.

"How long would I last?" She spoke bitterly. "The cops would grab me before the day was out."

"You've been on the blotter a few times, right?"

"So what?"

"You're right, you couldn't get away with it." He gave the message time to sink in before adding, "But a name, even if the right one, isn't necessarily proof—not the kind I need."

"I said I wouldn't testify."

"What kind of proof can you add?"

"You're trying to work it without paying me!" She tossed her head angrily.

"Would you expect me to pay that kind of money for just a name?"

"It should be worth something."

"Is the man still alive?" She jerked her head in a nod. He watched her, filling in his mental impressions. A hooker . . . a shabby room in a run-down neighborhood . . . access to pedestrian traffic. But there was something more, something in her eyes and manner that struck a distantly familiar note. Then it came to him: drugs. Although most of his career had been spent in traffic, he could recognize the symptoms; he'd seen enough drugged drivers for that. Bennies, nembies, speed, the Big H—it could be almost anything, but each left its shadow. "You seem to know him quite well," he pursued.

"Maybe." She glanced away.

"Where did you get your information?"

"None of your damned business!" She rose angrily. "Just like a fucking cop . . . trying to pump me."

"Trying to assess your information," he countered.

"You know it's true; the damned watch proves it."

"That you have knowledge of the crime, yes, but how much? I'm trying to establish a link between the watch and the name; that's what I need."

"That's your problem."

"Yours, too, if you're interested in the money."

"You're trying to get something for nothing; you never intended to pay." Her lips twisted malevolently. "You're just like all the other goddamned cops!" She turned and hurried from the room, slamming the door behind her.

Cassady slipped on his jacket and went to the window, saw her hastening toward the corner. Her quick, jerky steps mirrored her anger. Or fright. He thought of that while going down to his car. During their brief conversation the fright had never quite left her face—not even her anger or greed had masked it. The fright told him she wasn't a professional shakedown artist. Hooker, yes; drug addict, yes; but a rank amateur in her present league. A front . . . *for someone who knew*!

He followed her in his car, parking when she vanished into a nearby drugstore. Several minutes later she came out, halted at the curb, lit a cigarette and paced restlessly back and forth while waiting. In a short time a cab pulled alongside her and she got in.

Cassady tailed the cab, watching the back of her head through the rear window. She appeared to be sitting stiffly, eyes straight ahead, and he fancied she was clutching her purse tightly in her lap while struggling with her thoughts. He had no illusion that she'd surrendered the hope of getting the reward. Greed would win out; it almost always did. But for the present she'd reached an impasse she couldn't resolve and was going for advice to whoever had sent her.

He wasn't surprised when the cab passed through the main business district and turned onto East Fifth, an area of sleazy clothing stores, pawn shops, smoky counter cafes, adult movies, card rooms, porn shops—innumerable walk-up apartments in firetrap buildings which dated back to the turn of the century. Crime lived here in a thousand forms. So did the city's human failures, its downtrodden minorities, its impoverished and elderly. The city cared little about murder in the area—an indifference which gave crime the green light.

Cassady saw her lean forward to give directions; a moment later the cab pulled into a yellow zone and stopped. Cassady drove slowly past, found another slot and parked, watched in the rearview mirror as she turned in his direction. He averted his head as she passed. A dozen yards beyond she turned in at a narrow doorway, above which hung a faded sign that read *Golden Rooms*.

He felt certain she was meeting with whoever had sent

33

her. Possibly they lived together. Could her partner be one of Nancy's murderers, now trying to sell the other? If not, how much did they know? Their knowledge didn't stop with the watch; she'd admitted that. A name, she'd said. The right name, if they expected the reward. And they did. Their only problem was how to tie it down.

He sat unstirring, his mind automatically cataloguing the dilapidation and air of futility which lay like a suffocating cloud over the entire area—a background which exactly fitted that which he'd surmised for her. He could see her emerge after dusk . . . saunter beneath the lanes of yellow street lights . . . solicit the passing marines and sailors and less shabby of the civilians. Or perhaps she worked the nearby honky-tonks. The vice squad would know her well and so, perhaps, would the narcotics squad. Patterns in vice, like other behavioral patterns, varied but little in detail.

Dusk came slowly, blotting out the doorways, and the first neons began sending their calls into the night. From somewhere came the high thin wail of a sax against the low throb of drums. The tempo of the street was picking up. He was beginning to think she lived in the shabby apartment building when she emerged from the narrow doorway, turning in his direction. He glanced away until she had passed, then scrambled from the car and followed her.

She walked swiftly, glancing neither to the right nor left. Near the end of the block she turned in at another doorway. He flicked his eyes up to an all but illegible sign that read *Highland Apts*. He felt the keen anticipation of a traveler nearing the end of a weary journey.

Cassady halted momentarily before following her through the doorway. The diminishing clatter of her sandals on the wooden steps reached him and he saw her turn back toward the front of the building, then become lost to sight. Her own place, he was certain. And the other—the Golden Rooms—undoubtedly was where her accomplice lived. He felt a grim satisfaction.

A scream from above shattered the silence. Cassady took the stairs three at a time, reached the top as she stumbled toward him, her face twisted ugly with fright. Beyond her was a partially opened door. She jerked to a halt at the sight of him.

"They murdered him," she screamed, her voice strangled. Cassady dashed past her, hesitating only briefly as he heard her racing down the stairwell. She could be found quickly enough.

He moved swiftly through the doorway, halted abruptly at the sight of a bloody, half-naked figure lashed to a straight-back chair. He studied the scene with forced detachment. Legs, body and left arm were tightly bound; a sock was stuffed in the mouth and the bloody head, thrown back, revealed a cut throat; the scrawny chest and abdomen were a sea of gore. He glanced down; severed ears and nipples lay on the threadbare carpet.

Cassady stifled his nausea and moved closer. Scarred forearms bore angry, ulcerated sores that told of a long affair with the needle. Raw purplish splotches on the shoulders and those parts of the lower body not covered with blood puzzled him until his eyes lit on an ashtray containing half-burned tobacco from which the wrappings had been stripped away as if to remove any possible source of fingerprints. A pencil stub lay near the dead man's naked feet.

No stranger to violence, Cassady believed he saw more blood on the streets and highways in the course of a year than the average combat soldier did during his entire professional career. Nevertheless he felt sickened, not from the blood but from the manner in which the man had died. As he resurrected the scene, the gagged victim had been forced to write the answers to whatever questions had been asked. A sadistic murder, yes, but one performed coldly, with expertise in the ways of extracting information. Christ, a gangland kill, he felt certain.

He studied the body more closely—age, height, weight,

what he could see of the thin face. Subtract fifteen years and the victim could very well fit the physical description of either of Nancy's murderers. He had the enormous suspicion that this was one of them.

Quickly but carefully he inspected the shabby apartment. A worn wallet in a bureau drawer held a long-expired driver's license bearing the name of Frank H. Skousen; the face in the accompanying photograph was that of the dead man. At the time the license had been issued, nine years before, his age had been listed as twenty-five. It also gave an East Seventh Street address—useless, now, Cassady was certain. He found a scattering of other cards, dog-eared and soiled from age, but nothing he believed significant. Nevertheless, he jotted the information in a small black notebook before inspecting the rest of the apartment. A small closet held both male and female attire, all old, dirty, shabby. The squalid kitchenette, little more than a cubicle, contained a hotplate and a grimy sink filled with dirty dishes. A door led to an equally filthy bathroom.

With a last look at the dead man's face, he went downstairs to locate a phone.

Flash was cruising along East Fifth when he saw Lois burst from the doorway of the Highland Apartments. Alerted by the quick, fearful look she cast behind her before she fled toward Broadway, he sensed trouble and followed her, hoping it was something he might be able to translate into cash. The narcs? He glanced behind him, visibly relieved to find no one at his heels.

When she turned in at the dilapidated building where Bennie lived, he paused thoughtfully. Why the frantic rush? Had Skousen blown his top . . . threatened to beat her up? That couldn't be it; even Lois could whip that poor bastard. But how did Bennie fit into the picture?

He stood in front of Dave's Cafe and watched the doorway across the street. Maybe she hadn't paid her protection for the week. If so, the Syndicate could have sent someone to slap her around, get her back in line, but that still wouldn't explain her frantic flight to Bennie's. Could Frankie have gotten an overdose? He rejected the possibility immediately—Bennie cut the stuff too much for that. Give him five percent and he'd sugar it down to two, even less. Whatever it was, she was damned scared, and Bennie had to be in on it; that sounded like something that could be converted into cash. Christ, if he got Bennie over a barrel he could really bleed him.

His thoughts were broken as Lois ran out from the doorway. Looking fearfully toward the Highland Apartments, she turned and hurried away in the opposite direction.

Flash started to follow her, halting as he saw Bennie rush outside lugging a battered suitcase. *Bennie on the run!* Flash felt the excitement well inside him. Whatever had happened was big . . . big.

Bennie swiveled his gaze jerkily around before scurrying in the same direction taken by Lois. Flash followed a short distance behind. Lois turned left at the next intersection; when Bennie reached it, he turned to the right. Mentally toting up where the most profit might lie, Flash followed the dumpy figure.

"Why the goddamned torture?" Angelo Geraci glared angrily at Pinto across the top of his polished desk. "Why didn't you just kill the bastard, get out of there before the girl came?"

"What if he'd already squawked?" Short and thin, with small black eyes set in a narrow face, Pinto returned his gaze imperturbably. "You'd want to know that, wouldn't you, Angie?"

"Did he?" Geraci was suddenly still.

"Yeah, to the hooker he was shacked up with and to some goddamned pusher named Bennie . . . Bennie the Needle."

"Then why didn't you kill her?"

"No chance."

"Why not, for Christ's sake? She walked in on you, didn't she?"

"I was watching for her through the window . . . saw some goddamned cop right on her tail."

"Cop?" Geraci tried to hide his alarm.

"In plain clothes but still a cop. I can smell those bastards for a mile."

"Following the hooker? You know that?"

"No mistake. That's when I went out the back way, and fast."

"Any idea why he was following her?"

"A hooker? Sure, those guys are always trying to shake the babes down."

"I want her dead," Geraci said stonily. "I want her dead yesterday."

"Don't worry, she can't stay out of sight long."

"Any time is too long."

"I'll spread the word, turn some of the boys loose."

"This is strictly private, Pinto. I don't want any damned whispers getting around. First thing you know, some damned snitch will be whispering in a cop's ear. I can't afford that kind of crap."

"They won't know why we want her, Angie."

"Make damned sure of that." Geraci drummed his fingers against the desk. Christ knows how much Skousen had told the broad . . . and that Bennie, whatever-his-name was. A dozen good years, now everything was coming apart. He tried to stem his dismay. The cop following the hooker . . . Cassady? Unlikely, but safer to assume that it was.

He tried to put the possible action together in his mind,

work out a hypothesis that would explain what Pinto had told him. It seemed likely that she'd tried to make the sale but the cop hadn't bought, instead had tailed her back to her room. A cagey bastard, but he still wouldn't know. Not everything. Now Skousen was dead. That left Bennie, the hooker . . . the cop. He had to nip that, and damned fast.

Geraci brought his gaze back to Pinto's thin face. "I also want that Bennie."

"I figured that."

"He cut out owing us a bundle; tell the boys that."

"No trouble, Angie."

"The cop's name is Cassady . . . Sam Cassady. He's a sergeant in the Traffic Division."

"Yeah, I read the paper."

"I want him dead."

"You wanta bring down the fuckin' house?"

"You getting soft, Pinto?" Geraci leaned toward him. "You want I should get someone else?"

"You know better than that, Angie, but we damned well better make it look like an accident . . . or maybe a mugging or something."

"You make it look like that, Pinto; I don't want to know a thing about it."

"If Cassady's nosing around the street . . ."

"Figure it out, Pinto, figure it out."

"Which one first?"

"Both by yesterday. No, all three." Geraci folded his hands together and leaned back. "Let's have some fast action, and keep in touch." He gestured dismissal.

"Will do . . ." Pinto rose leisurely—arrogantly was the word that struck Geraci—and turned toward the door. Watching him leave, the enormity of his order struck him. Pinto was right—killing the cop could blow the town wide open. The news media would have a field day, especially if they sniffed a Syndicate involvement. Could Cassady's murder be tied to Skousen's? Only indirectly. No more than innuendo. Even so, the shit could really hit the fan. The Old Man would never sit still for that kind of publicity. No way.

He contemplated that uneasily. But he'd never know; not if Pinto handled it right. An accident. Some hyped-up punk with a switchblade. Happened all the time. Besides, he'd had no choice. Cassady was a fucking bird dog; his sticking to the scent all these years proved that. He'd never stop. What he didn't know now he might learn next week or the week after. Or next year. Jesus, fifteen years since the chick got it, and look at him now, breathing right down his neck. Twenty-five thousand—probably a phony offer but he'd gotten a bite. And if that had failed, what might he have tried next? He'd keep on and on.

Momentarily he entertained a vision of Cassady—the photo he'd seen in the newspaper. Not too smart or he wouldn't be stuck with traffic. Big and tough, that was all, but not too tough for Angelo Geraci. The reflection brought a small satisfaction. Years ago he would have taken care of the cop himself, with scarcely a second thought; but back then he'd had nothing to lose. Now with his position, money, power—and the respect that those things bought—he *was* somebody.

He felt his anger rise. Now a goddamned hooker, a pusher and a crummy cop were threatening to blow it all. Well, they'd asked for it. He contemplated his orders to Pinto, enjoying the sense of power. He had to be somebody to pass orders like that and know they'd be carried out without question. I say, do it—as simple as that. But turning the boys loose. . . . The reflection bothered him. Although he didn't like the idea one damned bit, he had to acknowledge that Pinto was right; they had to act fast. Neither would Pinto's men know the real reason for the search, nor were they stupid enough to get curious. That was the safety factor. When it came to that, Pinto was the cut-off; if the worst came to the worst, the well-known buck would stop there. And yet . . .

Geraci frowned. Bad enough that Pinto knew. But he was closemouthed, had to be; his own neck was right there on the line. Not that it seemed to bother him. He was like a damned machine—that methodical. He'd do the job, all right; still, he'd always have that bit of knowledge. That, Geraci decided, was what really bothered him. Knowledge, itself, was power; he'd have to consider that.

Pinto had to go—the thought came unbidden. Close that link and Geraci would be forever free. The total solution. That was the safest way, the only way. He breathed easier. He'd take care of that as soon as Cassady was dead. And Bennie and the hooker.

Geraci forced a faint smile, wondering if Pinto ever suspected just how expendable he was. Handle it right and the whole mess could be laid on Pinto's shoulders. It was the kind of move the Old Man might applaud. The kind of thing that set him apart from others, he reflected. Christ, he'd started even with guys like Skousen, and look at them now—down there scrounging. Damned few lifted themselves the way he had.

He lit a cigar and leaned back, his mind on the early years when, shortly after the shooting, he'd caught on working for a bookie. A crummy job but through it he'd met Big Joe Orkie, who'd damned soon recognized his talents. Loan sharking, gambling, narcotics, prostitution—he'd moved through the ranks slowly but surely, then unaccountably Big Joe had switched him to a job with a small finance company. He hadn't asked questions; if Big Joe thought it was the job for him, he was certain it would lead somewhere. And it had. During that period he'd learned his talents for organization, finance, the intricacies of handling invest-ments. Then he'd come to the Old Man's attention.

The Old Man! Although Geraci had met him but once,

that single meeting still burned in his mind. Close to sixty, gray, face seamed, a hawkish nose, very dark, probing eyes—that was the image that remained with him. In some strange manner the frail body had seemed to exude a terrible strength. So had the gentle voice.

Geraci had never known the Old Man's name, or where he lived, or what kind of life he led. He'd been taken to a shabby office—in what building, he didn't know—late at night in the back seat of a black Cadillac. Two exceedingly taciturn men had flanked him on either side. Although the mystery surrounding the Old Man had bothered him, he'd known better than to make inquiries. For several years, though, he'd scanned the daily financial and society sections in an attempt to glimpse the frail figure and thus give it identity. All such attempts had proved futile.

But when they'd first met, Geraci hadn't contemplated that; he could think of nothing but that his entire future was being weighed. With a word, a nod, the Old Man could consign him to the filthy neighborhood from which he'd come or he could propel him upward through the intricacies of the Syndicate to a position of wealth and power, as he had.

The Old Man's first question had been to the point. Vividly he recalled the soft voice asking, "Have you ever killed a man?"

Startled, he'd jerked his head in a negative before he found voice and said, "No, Sir."

"A woman?" Sensing the Old Man knew, he nodded affirmatively and started to explain. The Old Man silenced him with a gesture. "No details, please."

"Only to you," Geraci said hastily.

"Not even to me." The dark probing eyes were chiding. "That responsibility I shouldn't have."

Geraci cursed himself silently, certain he'd failed the test. Other questions followed, inconsequential in his view. His school, his parents' names, their background . . . how long from the Old Country? He responded briefly, politely, having concluded that the Old Man already knew the answers, that the whole interview had been set up to see how he'd respond to that one question about the woman. (*But how had he known about her?*) That question had never ceased to plague him.

Afterward he'd been dismissed, returned home in the same manner in which he'd arrived—sitting between two taciturn men in the rear of a black Cadillac.

But he hadn't failed! Within the week Big Joe Orkie had directed him to the office of Martin Tibbler, vice president of the Western Investment & Finance Company. Orkie's voice, when he'd given the order, had been unaccountably subdued and had carried a note of respect absolutely foreign to Geraci. It was at that moment that he realized he hadn't failed.

Martin Tibbler was small, graying, every bit the banker in his dark, conservative suit, tailored to fit his slender figure. His facial structure, urbane and patrician, was in stark contrast to his gray chill eyes. Sitting in his lavish office, they'd gone through brief amenities before Tibbler had offered him a position as assistant manager. Geraci had quickly accepted.

He'd learned early that his job was neither to assist Tibbler nor to aid in management, but merely to absorb the finer intricacies of finance. For weeks his only visitors had been lawyers and accountants, well-tailored, soft-voiced men who made suggestions, gave advice, warned of pitfalls in making loans, taught him the ways of the managerial arts—the thousand tributaries in the great flow of money.

Geraci had decided that this firm was legitimate, at least in its visible business. Loans at the highest legal rate of interest were made to individuals and small and large businesses; collateral took the form of first and second trust deeds, all protected by large margins of value and by maximum prepayment and late charge penalties. In that respect

43

it differed little from the city's scores of mortgage and finance companies. Geraci was satisfied; he knew he was being groomed for bigger things.

New visitors came, unidentified, but again he placed them as lawyers and accountants. From them he learned more about money—its dark side. It came in many forms, was laundered, slipped like quicksilver through ledgers and computers and from company to company, making strange transformations in the process. Profits were diminished, identified as capital outlay; assets became liabilities. The legal facade of one business would mask the highly illegal operations of another. Much of the money, he suspected, came from powerful pension funds, but the trail was murky, sensed rather than known. Vast housing developments, shopping centers, land investments—the money seeped everywhere, all legitimate by the books, all returning huge profits. Much of these, in turn, were dissipated in strange ways, their ultimate disposition unknown to him.

Through all the learning Geraci knew he was still being tested; knew, too, he was under almost constant surveillance. He'd come to know the several cars that tailed him regularly, recognized several of the same patrons in different restaurants where he dined. He had no doubt that his phones were tapped, his apartment bugged. Through it all he gave not the slightest indication that he knew there were eyes on him or listening ears. He forced himself to a life style as circumspect and discreet as that he attributed to Martin Tibbler. And to the Old Man.

Ten months later he was made president of Southwest Investment Enterprises, given a substantial raise, and moved to his present plush offices, fourteen floors above where Martin Tibbler labored in his vineyard. Other men, not so soft-spoken, came to coach him on the company's operations. The surface business still centered on loans, all legal, backed by books which would pass the most meticulous scrutiny. It also served as a holding company for firms which bid against each other for the city's lucrative paving, sewer and construction contracts. But the company's real function was as a conduit through which flowed immense amounts of money from gambling, prostitution, loan shark operations, narcotics and pornography. Recorded on microfilm, the money flowed out through another conduit—to where, Geraci didn't know. Neither did he know the disposition of the microfilm after it passed into Martin Tibbler's personal care.

Geraci also was made aware of another small branch of the company which, not so strangely, appeared neither on its table of organization nor its payroll. In it were men he knew well—not personally, at first, but because they echoed the ghetto streets of his youth. Brutal men, killers if need be, but necessary. Geraci, for the first time, felt at home.

Since then his power had grown enormously. At times he managed to forget that such a person as the Old Man existed, and fancied himself at the top of the pyramid. But he would quickly disillusion himself, knowing he was but a cog in an immense machine. But an important cog. And the Old Man *was* old. Maybe someday. . . . Now a lousy cop was threatening to fuck him up. Cassady—a goddamned Mick. Well, Pinto would take care of that.

Geraci smiled. A singularly unpleasant smile.

4

"Lois Wilson has a record as long as your arm," Inspector Marcos Garmont told Cassady. "Mainly prostitution and drug offenses. She's also been booked under the names Louise Wilton and Anita Wilcox."

"I noticed that." Cassady waited for the other to continue. Tall and angular, with thick dark hair framing a lean, slightly askew face that denied his more than fifty years, Garmont fitted the well-worn term: a cop's cop. Cassady held him in the highest esteem.

"It's somewhat of a pattern with women," Garmont reflected. "When they take a phony name, it usually holds the ring of their real one . . . perhaps a subconscious attempt to hold on to their identity."

"She's in this up to her neck," Cassady declared.

"In the attempt to get the reward, yes, but how much does she really know?"

"Enough to get Skousen murdered."

"Agreed, Sam. Tell me what you think."

"That murder was a Syndicate job. I might be a traffic man, but I know enough to know that."

"We've concluded that, but as yet we have to prove it. That's always the hang-up, isn't it?"

Cassady leaned toward him. "An order like that would have had to come from the top. Can you imagine anyone that high throwing that spotlight on the Syndicate unless his own neck was in the noose? The killer might as well have left a Syndicate calling card."

"True," Garmont murmured.

"Someone up there panicked, Marcos."

"You're talking around the edges, Sam."

"No, I'm not." He shook his head. "I'm saying that Skousen was one of Nancy's murderers; the second was Mr. Big in the Syndicate. He saw the story, knew he had to get rid of Skousen, but he also knew he had to first find out if Skousen had already blabbed."

"Accomplices," Garmont prodded. "A down-at-the-heels junkie and a high up Syndicate figure?"

"That doesn't tell us the situation fifteen years ago."

"True, they could have been close once, but there's nothing on the record to indicate that Skousen was ever anything but a typical end-of-the-road loner. He came out of high school, began building his drug record a year later."

"There was that year," objected Cassady. He knew Garmont was deliberately drawing him out, a technique he had.

"There's that, yes." Garmont rustled with a sheet on his desk. "Bennie Worth's the puzzle."

Bennie Worth . . . Bennie the Needle. Cassady reviewed the profile he'd gotten of him. A failed con artist, now a hype who supported his habit by pushing. He'd been in and out of jail a dozen times since graduating from the Youth Authority. The mug shot showed a narrow, almost cheekless face with an abnormally long, pointed nose—easy to remember. The full-length was of a lumpy, ungainly body—a man made of disparate parts. Narcotics had had Bennie's apartment staked out for a couple of weeks. Skousen had

48

been a regular visitor; the woman less so, but several times had stayed overnight. Now Bennie, no doubt warned by Lois, was on the run.

"Bennie and the woman were working it together," Cassady said.

"That's reasonable."

"Do you think Bennie could have killed Skousen?"

"No way, Sam. Worth's record doesn't indicate that kind of violence. Men like him are jackals; torture-murder isn't their line. If he'd wanted to get rid of Skousen, a simple overdose would have served nicely. But he might be the key to the whole mess; we'll pick him up fast."

"It has to be damned fast," Cassady objected. "The same with Skousen's babe. They're a danger to someone and I have to get them before that someone does . . . find out what they know. I shouldn't have let the woman get away," he added ruefully.

"She won't be loose long," Garmont predicted. "A gal like that has a high visibility factor. She has to peddle to live and she'll need her fix regularly. We have plenty of eyes and ears down there."

"So does the Syndicate."

Garmont's eyes took on a faraway look. "There's still the question of how much she knows . . . the danger she presents. She could have been working in the near-blind."

"She knew about the watch . . . claims to know a name."

"She had to be told that much to convince you, but who told her? Skousen? Bennie? A third party?"

"Does it matter, Marcos? She's part of the chain; that's good enough for me." Cassady rubbed his jaw. "I'm positive Skousen was my man . . . one of them. A gut feeling. But when he was killed he was already down the drain. I can't imagine him trying to collect."

Garmont waited.

"He was a clay pigeon," Cassady pursued. "Maybe the gal got the story from him, was getting ready to sell him down the river, but I know she wasn't expecting him to get murdered. You'd know that if you'd heard her scream, seen the terror on her face."

He paused, resurrecting a picture of the brief scene. He couldn't remember ever having seen another human so frightened, so panicked. But the panic was the key; it had not been occasioned by the brutal murder so much as what it might portend for her; he felt certain of that.

"Keep going," Garmont encouraged.

"She and Bennie were after the money, but that wasn't the case with the killer," he pursued. "That job was to discover how much Skousen might have blabbed . . . and to whom . . . and to silence him. That puts the gal right on the spot, along with Bennie. His sudden flight is evidence of that. Hell, he left most if not all of his personal belongings behind. That spells Syndicate. What else could have panicked them like that? When Skousen got it, they both knew they were next—maybe even knew the punk who did it."

"Not a punk, Sam."

"Okay, a hit man." Cassady lifted his eyes. "You have a candidate?"

"A suspect." Garmont smiled mirthlessly. "He was playing cards with a couple of his buddies at the time. Aren't they always?"

"What's his name?"

"Luigi Pinto, by the records. Don't worry, Sam, we'll nail him."

Cassady conjured up a vision of the kind of man who could butcher another like that, then a second figure materialized in the background—a shadowy image of the nameless somebody who had ordered the murder. That was the man he wanted. "Whose man is Pinto?"

"It could be any of several men, Sam. Those names are lost in the clouds."

"But you know them?"

"Of them," Garmont corrected. "The only ones we're

50

really certain of are those at street level . . . the working stiffs."

"Who's the main one?"

"At street level? Joe Orkie, but he's still a working stiff. Not that he punches a time clock."

"What about him?"

"He runs a trucking firm over on Alameda, the corner of 22nd Street. That part of the business appears legitimate. But Orkie's out—he didn't order that job."

"Why so certain?"

"That's not Orkie's style, Sam. Sure, his men punch a few people around when they're late in their payments, things like that, and possibly there's a hit now and then, but not torture murder. The Syndicate keeps a damned low profile, Sam. Orkie's the last visible face of the working mob, and even that we can't prove. His job is to keep it that way—a cut-off, you might say. He'd be the last one to bring the Syndicate into that kind of exposure."

"Who's above him?"

Garmont shook his head. "Do you want the names of corporation presidents, board chairmen . . . men against whom we haven't a shred of evidence? Knowing and proving are two different cats, Sam. You're a cop; you know that. Besides, there are other considerations."

"Such as?"

"Twenty-five thousand makes a pretty fair bundle, Sam. Someone—let's say Pinto—might have been trying to dig up enough information to collect it." Garmont's eyes said he didn't believe that.

"That doesn't grab me, Marcos."

"I didn't think it would." Garmont eyed the younger man reminiscently. Long years before, he'd tabbed Cassady as a real comer. A sergeant at the time, he'd sized Cassady up as a future inspector, possibly even an assistant chief or chief. But all that had vanished in the crash of gunfire that had taken the life of his young wife. The brilliance hadn't

51

faded, but Cassady had turned inward. Although he continued to perform his duties with far above average competence, the spark that drove men to the top had died. So had his ambition. Now, Garmont could sense that spark burning brightly again.

Cassady's head came up. "I've got a couple of weeks on the books. I'd like to take the time off."

"To pursue this thing?" Garmont shook his head.

"Look, I'm close to whoever killed Nancy; I feel that in my bones. Skousen was in on it and his partner's still around; the killing indicates that. I won't let the bastard get away."

"I can sympathize with you, Sam."

"I can feel a however coming."

"I'm sorry, but you're right. Your training and experience don't qualify you for this kind of thing. You're a traffic man. This is a job for homicide, narcotics, vice. They have a thousand eyes and ears down there. They'll pull in your Bennie and little Lois fast enough."

"I've waited fifteen years, Marcos. I want in."

"No go, Sam."

"Then I'll turn in my badge, do it my way."

"What could you hope to accomplish as a private citizen?"

"I'd satisfy myself that I'd done all I could. After that I'd sleep nights—live again."

Garmont studied him. "A personal question, Sam."

"Shoot."

"What do you really want, justice or revenge?"

"Justice, as you damned well know!" Cassady flushed.

"I'm not that certain; you're too anxious to get in on the kill."

"I won't let that bastard get away, if that's what you mean. I told you that."

"Think about it, that's all I'm asking you."

"I have, Marcos, for a long time."

"Okay, put in for your leave."

"Effective immediately," Cassady urged. "I have the feeling that every hour counts."

"I'll push the paper. . . . And good luck, Sam."

"Thanks, Marcos." Cassady rose, fuming inwardly as he turned toward the door. What he didn't need was a lecture about motive.

Watching him leave, a small smile crinkled the corners of Garmont's mouth. It was, he thought, like watching a man be born again.

Cassady got the call that evening.

Her voice was tense, edged with panic, and he conjured up an image of her huddled in a dark phone booth somewhere, glancing worriedly around as she spoke. *Someone was out to get her. . . . She needed money. . . . She had to get out of town*—the words came off in a frantic tone.

"Hop a cab; I'll be waiting," Cassady said.

"Please, can I trust you?" Not a whore's voice but that of a small girl.

"You can trust me." He sensed her hesitancy before he heard the click of the receiver. He replaced the instrument thoughtfully, certain she was ready to exchange information for safety. But she'd keep it to a minimum, or try. Still, she damned well knew she couldn't sell him the name of a dead man. Her terror? That could only stem from Skousen's partner. The man he wanted.

Cassady had the feeling he was very close. Skousen had sung her name, no doubt about that. Now she was slated for a cut throat, or believed she was. Corporation presidents and board chairmen—he'd be up there somewhere, among them. But her terror wouldn't stem from anyone so remote. It would come from Pinto, or someone like him.

He was getting in deep, he reflected, and he hadn't even started yet. What did he know about the Syndicate? That it existed—a few names, a swirl of whisper and rumor about payoffs, political ties, but that was all. The men in vice, narcotics, homicide, the special intelligence unit—they'd have it taped. So would Garmont. Now he'd cut himself off from Garmont's aid . . . from the department. The way he'd wanted it.

He went to the window to watch for her cab. But Garmont was right: he was a babe in the woods. He knew about slaughter on the streets and highways—head-ons, over-turned trailer rigs, drunken and dope-addled drivers, man-gled bodies. Occasionally he'd stumbled across a robbery in progress. But that and corralling crazy kids in stolen cars wasn't much of a school for untangling a fifteen-year-old murder. Or for batting heads with the Syndicate.

A cab drew up to the curb and Cassady automatically scanned the street behind it for a tail before he switched his gaze to the woman hastily exiting from the rear. Her distress was evident in the way she hurriedly fumbled in her purse, shoved some money toward the driver, bolted toward the entrance.

At the sound of the chimes he waited a full minute before answering the door to let her anxiety mount. When finally he opened it she was nervously extracting a cigarette from her purse. Her dark hair disheveled, her narrow face tight with fright, she wore the same wrinkled blue blouse, tan skirt and stained white sandals she had during her last visit. He stepped aside and invited her in.

She walked past him, lit the cigarette and turned. The dark eyes in their purple hollows held a haunted look. He gestured toward a chair. She glanced around suspiciously before perching on the edge of it, legs drawn up as before.

"Okay, let's have it," he said.

"I need money to get out of town." The words tumbled out abruptly, hysteria not far behind.

"What's the rush?"

"Someone's out to get me."

"Because of what you know?"

She jerked her head in a nod.

"Who?"

"I . . . don't know."

"The Syndicate?"

She started violently. "How . . . how do you know?"

"Take it easy; you're safe here."

"God . . ." She struggled with her thoughts, repeated the question.

"Your boyfriend's murder," Cassady said, "a typical Syndicate job."

"I . . . I . . ." She jerked her head up frightened, fumbling for words.

"As you damned well know," he finished.

"But I don't," she cried, "I don't know that!"

"No? You surprise me. I thought you had something to sell."

"A name, I told you . . . a name."

"I'm listening."

"Frankie . . ." She moistened her lips. "It was Frankie."

"Skousen, a dead man." He studied her coldly. "Do you expect me to pay for the name of a dead man?"

"You said . . ."

"Tell me about Bennie Worth," he barked.

"Bennie?" He caught the startled look in her eyes.

"Bennie the Needle, you know, up in the Golden Rooms . . . or was until he took off."

"Yeah, Bennie." He recognized the stall as she tried to put that one together. "Bennie, that's right," she said finally. She watched him anxiously.

"What about him?"

"Bennie did it."

"Did what?"

"Killed her . . . he and Frankie."

"And Bennie killed Skousen, right?"

"Yeah."

"Because Skousen was trying to sell him?"

"Yeah, that was it."

"How do you know?"

"Because, well . . ." She twisted her thin hands together. "Frankie told me about it, said Bennie had threatened him, then, when it happened . . . well, I know he did it."

"Bullshit!"

"What do you mean?" she flared angrily.

"Bennie was just a goddamned pusher. The two of you were trying to sell me Skousen, collect the money, right?"

"You're trying to trap me!" She sprang to her feet.

"You're already trapped."

"Trapped how?" Fear flooded her face. "I only told you what I heard and you can't prove it . . . can't prove nothin'!"

"You're trapped because you know what Bennie knows, what Skousen knew—the name of the second killer."

"You're guessing . . . trying to scare me."

"Am I? Why are you on the run? Think you can outrace the Syndicate? No way." He shook his head. "They'll tie you up like they did Skousen . . . use the knife."

"God . . . " Her hands shook uncontrollably as she tried to light another cigarette. Cassady felt like a heel but knew it was the only way he'd get her to talk. Just one word, a name . . . Finally she succeeded and drew the smoke deeply into her lungs while trying to collect her thoughts. She jerked her gaze back. "How . . . how do you know it was the Syndicate?"

"Like I said, the torture murder. We both know that. And we both know another thing: they won't stop with Skousen."

"You're trying to frighten me."

"Just giving you the facts."

"God, they're monsters," she whispered.

"Sure, and you're protecting them. Did that ever occur to you? By clamming up, you're writing your own death certificate."

"How long would I last if I talked?" she asked bitterly.

"You know how long you'll last if you don't talk." At her silence, he said, "You might have a way out, I don't know."

"How?" The word was laden with hope and doubt.

"If I had his name . . . bagged him before he got to you . . ."

"There'd be others."

"Not on this deal. If I bag him no one else would be damned fool enough to push it."

She hesitated. "And if I give a name?"

"I know a safe place where you can hide . . . stay out of sight until it's over."

"I won't testify, I told you that."

"If I dig up other proof you might not have to."

"I won't, that's final. God, I wouldn't last five minutes."

"It's your best chance . . . your only chance."

"How about the money?" The greed was back in her voice again.

"If the information proves out—if I nail him—you get it all."

"If it doesn't? If you know but can't prove it, what then?"

"I'll give you enough to move somewhere, get started again."

"How much?"

"Five thousand."

"I'd be trusting you. . . ."

"Look, sister, I could throw you to the wolves right now."

"How do I know you won't anyway?"

"You don't, but you still have to trust me."

"What about . . . the safe place?"

"A small motel on the edge of town. The Blue Sky; a friend runs it. Name's Cady . . . Lou Cady. I'll give him a call, send you out there in a cab."

"What am I supposed to use for money?"

"I'll have him put it on the cuff." He extracted several bills from his wallet and handed them to her. "There's a small cafe next door."

"I never thought I'd trust a goddamned cop," she said bitterly.

"But now you have to, right?"

"All right." She crushed her cigarette nervously in an ashtray, then forced her eyes back. "Geraci," she whispered, "Angelo Geraci."

Geraci . . . Angelo Geraci—the name echoed in Cassady's mind as he watched the cab carry Lois into the night. When it vanished from sight he went to the phone, spoke briefly with Lou Cady, then poured a stiff shot of bourbon and settled back to think.

What did he know about Geraci? The name rang a distant bell, but that was about all. He prided himself on his memory—a mishmash of trivia which over the years never seemed to escape and which occasionally served him well. Now he sorted through it to find what had rung the bell. Someone he'd ticketed? The question returned a deep void. Rumor? Whisper? Cop talk? Some chance remark? That last stirred something deep in his subconscious and he focused on it. Which chance remark? When? Where? Elusive memories flickered past like a motion picture on a high-speed-track.

"That fucking Geraci financed the twenty million . . ." The words came suddenly, and with it a vignette unfolded—Captain Hendel of the intelligence unit talking to Crane of vice when he'd passed them in the hall. How long ago? Several years, at least.

Cassady felt a stir of excitement. A man who could finance twenty million . . . Corporation presidents and board chairmen, Garmont had said. The thread tracked. At least Geraci would be easy to find.

He had an image of a bloody figure tied to a chair, another of a faceless, well-groomed man in an elegant air-conditioned office. Two radically different kinds of men from different worlds, light years apart in their life styles and social lives, yet linked by a mutual secret.

Cassady switched his mind to practical considerations. If the early years he'd postulated for Geraci were right, R & I undoubtedly would have some kind of a package on him. And if now in the Syndicate, Hendel would know him well. So, probably, would the brass in vice, in narcotics. And Garmont would know. He let the hopes fade. After blackjacking the inspector into leave, he couldn't lean on him now. It was his baby; he'd wanted it that way and now he had it. How could he reach the bastard, tie him to a fifteen-year-old murder, nail him to the mast? He needed information . . . a hell of a lot more than he'd gotten from Lois.

Bennie Worth? Maybe . . . Bennie knew something, enough to put him on the run. Enough to know it was a Syndicate job. He contemplated that. Bennie's own neck had to be on the block, which meant that he had dangerous knowledge—something threatening to whoever had ordered Skousen's murder? Geraci? The totality of information screamed "*Yes!*"

Find Bennie—that, he decided, was the first step. Follow Garmont's advice, start lower on the ladder. Get into Bennie's milieu. He'd be known to prostitutes, addicts, his suppliers. If he were a junkie himself, entirely probable, he'd be driven to contact other pushers. Someone would talk; someone would always talk . . . for a price.

He went to the bedroom and studied himself in the mirror. Christ, he looked like a cop, stood like a cop, smelled like a cop. The stamp was all over him. Neither did his rugged, weather-beaten face nor the wide shoulders and deep chest fit into Bennie's derelict world. The thick dark hair, graying at the temples, was far too short, too neat. Stop shaving, put on old clothes, and he might pass as a truck driver, a former second-rate pug, a bouncer in a honky-tonk.

Down to the ghetto. Find Bennie.

He gazed around the room. Sterile walls, sparse furnishings, shabby with neglect. Not a home—never had been;

merely a place to hang his hat. A place of escape, to shut out the world. Home—he hadn't had one since Nancy died. He felt the vacuum of the long years before he'd met Cindy. Occasional women, now nameless and faceless—no more than biological necessities. Television and books and eons of solitude, the way he'd wanted it. Until he'd met Cindy. Now all that was coming to an end; he'd have a home again. Cindy and two sons. But first there was Geraci.

He jerked his mind back to pragmatic things. Geraci would command power, muscle, have a thousand pipelines. He'd also have highly-placed friends in the city's social, economic and political power structures. Not a man to be underestimated. Within hours he'd know who was tracking Bennie, and why. And then? He visualized Skousen's bloody body again. The image gave him answer.

Cassady tried to place himself in Geraci's shoes. Three people, at least, might topple him from his place of power: Bennie, Lois . . . and himself. Geraci's response to any moves on his own part would be swift. But he and Geraci had one thing in common: they'd both be hunter and hunted.

He considered his own position. He had become a creature of habit. Leave in the morning, return in the evening, twice a week to the gym—a clockwork life. Now habit could kill him. Walk through the door into a gun with a silencer or a knife in the dark. There were a thousand ways to kill a man. All easy. He'd have to start from the beginning, shuck his habits, create a new Cassady, find a safe place to hole up in . . . cut himself off from everyone.

Find Bennie before Geraci did.

5

"BENNIE WORTH?" THE BARTENDER shook his head slowly while wiping his hands on a soiled towel. "Can't say that I know many of my customers by name."

"Bennie the Needle," Cassady prodded. "Does that ring a bell?" He caught the sudden wariness in the other's jowly face, the cessation of movement of the hands. Suspicion flooded the dark eyes.

"Can't say that it does." The bartender cast a quick look around and moved away, ostensibly to serve another customer. End interrogation, reflected Cassady, satisfied that at least the bartender knew Bennie. Or of him. Had the bartender taken him for a narc?

He studied his reflection in the mirror. Despite the stubbly beard that gave his jaw a bluish cast and the untidy dark hair, the cop was still there, but he suspected the real reason for the bartender's sharp reaction was that the Syndicate had passed the word: find Bennie. Bennie and Lois, he corrected. Geraci wouldn't rest easy while they were on the loose. Now word would be getting back to him: *Some big guy asking questions about Bennie . . . about six-one or -two, dressed like a bum, needs a shave . . .*

What would Geraci make of that? A cop? Probably. Although Cassady hated to believe it, he was certain that links existed between the police and crime families in almost every large city. By now Geraci probably knew the name of every cop working the case. Perhaps even his own. But if that information made him sweat, so much the better.

He returned his gaze to the whiskey in front of him. Rotgut! He emptied the contents of the glass on the floor and went outside, pausing to scan the street. Drab shops, counter cafes, cardrooms, adult bookstores, porn movies, narrow doorways which led to innumerable walk-up rooms—and somewhere in the warren around him, Bennie. He pictured the narrow face with its slack cheeks and needlelike nose, the lumpy body. A high visibility factor. He'd hole up under another name, damned well stay out of sight, yet he had to come out sometime—for food, if nothing else.

Cassady formed a grid in his mind, quartered it, decided on the southeast quadrant first. Starting from the vicinity of the Golden Rooms, he began questioning cab drivers, bartenders, waiters, hookers, pimps. Mostly he encountered a sudden wariness, suspicion, outright hostility—a probing by the eyes to assess who he was, what he wanted. At other times the reaction was fear, as if just knowledge of Bennie somehow was a personal threat.

Within a few hours he began to appreciate the magnitude of his job. He'd covered scores of places, was still within several blocks from where he'd started. By now the suspicious look, the quick denial, were becoming the expected response. He marveled at how quickly the Syndicate had spread the word. About him, too—he sensed that in the reactions he'd received. *The big guy* . . . Probably dozens of eyes had watched his passage.

His attention was drawn to a woman standing in the shelter of a doorway, smoking as she eyed the passersby. Her face was an open invitation. Thin, dark hair a mess, shabby dress, middle thirties . . . a hooker getting an early start. He made the assessment automatically.

She caught his eyes as he approached; a painted smile revealed several missing teeth. "Looking for someone?" Her voice held a cajoling note.

"Bennie Worth . . . Bennie the Needle. Seen him around?"

"That goddamned Bennie! You a cop?"

"No, he ripped off a friend."

"That motherfucker would."

Cassady let the edge of a five-dollar bill show. "Seen him?"

"No, but plenty of people are asking." She eyed the money. "I like the color." He opened his palm. She plucked the bill from it and tucked it into her bra.

"What do you tell them?"

"He's gone. If the people who are looking for him can't find him, he's really gone. A goddamned good thing, too."

"Gone where?"

"Wherever rats go. Who knows in this goddamned world?"

"Who's looking for him?"

"The cops . . . everyone."

"Who's everyone?"

"Think I'm crazy? Don't ask."

"The Syndicate?"

"You said it, I didn't."

"Are they looking for anyone else?"

"Maybe." She looked down at his hand again. Cassady brought out another five-dollar bill, watched the nimble fingers dispose of it before she said, "A woman named Lois Wilson."

He switched the subject. "You're not supposed to talk, are you?"

"Am I talking? I haven't said a thing."

"Thanks, anyway."

"Sure you wouldn't like a romp? I've got a room upstairs."

"Maybe next time . . ." He moved away, heartened that one person, at least, hadn't been afraid to speak out, if only by indirection. Geraci's men had covered the ground, their message loud and clear: *Don't talk!* Or maybe it was *Don't talk to the big guy*. And who on this miserable street would buck the Syndicate? Not many. Yet the woman had given him hope.

How would Lew Archer handle this one? The reflection made him smile. Archer would go on and on, like he always did, until he bagged his man. Or until MacDonald devised some way for Archer to bag him. Great, except that he had no MacDonald to guide him.

His thoughts turned sober. Garmont was right, this was a job for the men in homicide, narcotics, vice. They already knew most of the faces in the warrens around him, had an army of snitches. He contemplated that. Now they'd be working around the clock; the howl raised in the press by the torture-murder ensured that. How much did they know by now? A morning editorial, blasting the police and courts alike for the increasing lawlessness in the streets, had attributed the brutal slaying to the Syndicate. Lt. Dom Perrotti of Homicide, denying knowledge of such a link, had branded that pure speculation. But Perrotti would play it close to the vest. Yet, totaled, they still had nothing. The knowledge gave him a curious satisfaction. Geraci was his baby; he'd nail him if he had to tear the goddamned Syndicate apart to do it.

How far flung was Geraci's net? The question gave him pause. It covered the sprawling east side, certainly, but it couldn't extend far beyond that. Not an escape-proof net. Had Bennie outrun it? He considered the man's background, character, need for others of his kind, and decided against the possibility. This was Bennie's world; he'd seek his refuge in it.

Several hours later, tired, hot, his feet aching, he stopped for coffee. Sitting at a drab counter, he wondered if there was something he might be missing, some angle overlooked. Lois! He cursed softly. He hadn't asked her about Bennie's friends or where he might be hiding. If she knew his friends, would name just one . . . On impulse he sought out a pay phone in the cafe.

"Blue Sky Motel." Lou Cady's voice held the reassuring note of motel managers everywhere.

"Cassady," he said.

"Sam?" The name jumped out in a sharp exclamation. "I've been trying to reach you."

"I've taken a downtown room for a while. What's wrong?" Cady wasn't one to be perturbed easily.

"Your bird's flown."

"When?"

"She took off this morning, hasn't returned; I've had the maid checking. She said she saw her at the phone early, probably calling a cab."

Cassady digested the information. When he'd stashed her away at the motel, he'd felt certain her fear would keep her there. Christ! Suddenly he realized his mistake. The monkey! The goddamned monkey! He told Cady. "Now she's out hooking to feed it," he said.

"Think she'll be back?"

"If she's lucky, Lou." They exchanged a few more words before Cassady replaced the phone. You're a stupid bastard, he told himself. He'd given her plenty to eat on, but not enough to feed a goddamned monkey. Anyone in the narcotics squad could have told him what would happen. *Out on the street . . . hooking . . . and where would she go*? Yeah, right back to her own bailiwick—the bars and dark doorways and walk-up rooms she knew best—exactly where Geraci's thousand eyes would be. Grudgingly he admitted she would have no choice; her slovenly dress and worn body wouldn't bring her a nickel in the better neighborhoods. *How many tricks to feed a hungry monkey*? Jesus, he didn't even know the economics of that one.

He finished his second cup of coffee and went outside. The late afternoon heat, boiling down through a smoggy sky, struck him as fiercer than ever.

"Looking for a girl?" The sibilant whisper brought Cassady around sharply. A slender black man of around thirty waited inside a recessed doorway. He wore a yellow shirt, blue blazer jacket, matching slacks with a knife-edge crease, blue suede shoes. The dark eyes in the thin, handsome face were sharp, calculating.

Cassady shook his head and stepped closer. "A guy named Bennie."

"Bennie?"

"Bennie Worth, he's . . ."

"Oh, Bennie the Needle. He's hot, man, hot. You a cop? Not that I give a fuck. Another guy asked me that, man . . . laid on a tenner. The layin' on of hands, man, I love it."

Cassady felt a flare of hope. Drawing a ten-dollar bill from his wallet, he watched it snatched by brown fingers. "What did you tell him?"

"Down that way, man." The slim Negro pointed. "The Golden Rooms, ya can't miss it."

"Yeah, that's where he used to live."

"He's gone, man? He must've really ripped someone off."

"You said he was hot."

"Like fire, man."

"How do you know?"

"A ten don't buy much, man."

Cassady brought out another bill, watched it snatched away. "Who's after him?"

"Like everyone, man. He must have ripped off his supplier . . . a big one. Even the fuzz are out . . . a fuckin' battalion. The hot line's hittin' the snitches."

"The cops wouldn't be after him for that."

"The cops and everyone else, man. Like I said, Bennie's hot."

"Who else?"

"Man, I don't get my throat cut for two dinky tens. No way, man."

Cassady extracted a twenty from his wallet, held it firmly. "Who else?"

"Ya goin' to let go of that piece of paper?"

"If I get the right answer, yeah."

"The Syndicate, man, the fuckin' Syndicate."

"Who in the Syndicate?"

"A thin guy, short, maybe forty—wears a dark snapbrim hat, sharp threads; that's all I know, man."

"His name?"

"No name, man."

"Thanks." Cassady relinquished the bill. "I'm in the market if you happen to hear the name. I'll be around."

"I'll listen, man." The pimp opened the door, retreated up the stairs. Cassady tilted his head upward; a faded sign read *Omega Rooms*. He didn't think he'd been ripped off. The Syndicate—no surprise there; but the thin man . . . Skousen's murderer? Christ, he hadn't even thought to ask Garmont for Pinto's description. Great going. What else hadn't he asked? He was beginning to appreciate Garmont's views about his training and background. A traffic cop. Still, no one was ahead of him. Not yet. But he had to get moving. If the Syndicate—the thin man!—got to Bennie first, Geraci could laugh at the charge. But he won't, he promised himself.

Short, thin, about forty, wears a dark snapbrim hat—he tucked the information away, satisfied. Again he'd proved that not everyone on Geraci's home turf was immune to the blandishments of a few bucks. Pimps, pushers, hookers, cab drivers, bartenders—they all lived in the tempo of the streets, antennae constantly attuned. The payoff was survival, money, or both. It was just a matter of finding the right person; that and a loaded wallet. He moved on.

Later he had supper in another cafe, a hole in the wall;

no name, six stools and from the outside it looked fairly clean. When he came out it was dusk. Where had the hours gone? How much ground had he covered? A few square blocks. At his present rate the search would take him weeks. A discouraging thought. The first street lights came on, yellowish in the smoggy air. Perhaps the darkness would help, provide a reassuring anonymity.

Walking the dark side streets, he kept close to the curbs, aware at how swiftly a hand with a loaded blackjack could strike out from a recessed doorway. Several times small groups of young punks watched him speculatively, let him pass. He kept his ears attuned for the sound of movement behind while he searched the dark shadows ahead and to the sides. Marines, sailors, hookers, pimps, muggers—a goddamned jungle. And somewhere in it, Bennie. Yeah, and Lois.

His back against a building, he scanned the darkness.

"Lookin' for someone, honey?" A black woman edged out from a doorway, half lost in shadow.

Cassady halted. "Yeah, a guy named Bennie . . . Bennie the Needle."

"Bennie?" Fright in her voice, she stood for a moment as if frozen before abruptly retreating inside. A towering figure took her place, blocked the entrance. The sharp snick of a switchblade came again.

"Keep movin', man."

"Peace." Cassady made a "V" with his fingers and continued on. Big Boy wasn't about to talk about Bennie, that was for sure. No chance for wallet diplomacy. By now he was probably grabbing a phone to report to someone.

The idea gave rise to another message: Probably a lot of them had reported the contact. He had a mental image of Geraci sticking colored pins in a map and saying, " . . . *and in about ten minutes he'll be. . . .*" He suppressed a smile; it wasn't that funny. Chart his path and he'd be ripe for the plucking. He'd have to watch that one.

By midnight he was back on East Fifth. His eyes roved. Flashing neons, lighted cafes and bars; the marquees of all-night porn shows glittered. Pedestrians—singly, in couples, small groups. Mostly men. A prowl car wheeled past, its red and amber lights swirling. From somewhere came the crash of drums. In contrast to the dark and nearly deserted side streets, the tempo of life was here unabated.

One day gone. What accomplishment could he measure against it? What had he learned for the scores of people he'd interrogated? Almost nothing. He had a name, Angelo Geraci—that was a big plus; but against it he had a minus: he'd lost Lois. Maybe tomorrow would be better.

He was headed back toward the shabby room he'd rented when he glimpsed a figure behind him—a momentary reflection in the angled window of a junk shop. His impression had been of a small man, dark clothes, a hat; he'd seemed to glide rather than walk.

Cassady moved ahead without pausing, letting the impression burn in his mind. He listened for footsteps, a change of pace, heard nothing but the normal sounds of the night, yet knew the slight figure was still behind him; some sense, somewhere deep in his mind, shouted that. Moves like a damned cat, he thought.

At the angled window of a pawnshop he halted casually, as if to view the display, saw the mirrored figure break stride, step suddenly into a doorway. The abruptness of the move came like a flashing red signal. A snitch following him to a safe place to try to peddle information? A punk looking for a mark? One of the Syndicate's eyes? More likely the latter. If so, his inquiries about Bennie were drawing a quick response. He smiled to himself.

He continued on for several blocks without looking back, but with the persistent sense of being followed. Abruptly he turned onto a dimly-lit side street and a few paces farther stepped into a dark doorway to scan the intersection behind him. A drunk lurched across the street, followed by a bedraggled old crone clutching a white shawl close to her throat.

Perhaps thirty seconds later another figure came into view at the far side of the intersection, scanned the dark street in Cassady's direction—a surveillance that was quick, probing, before he suddenly retreated.

Short, thin, a dark snapbrim hat . . . the other had been tailored to the pimp's description. The Syndicate's man! Cassady edged back through the shadows and peered around the corner; the other was lost to sight.

He contemplated the sequence of actions: the thin man's caution in approaching the intersection from the far side, his quick scrutiny and sudden retreat. He'd sensed Cassady's awareness of him, had seen the dark street as a trap. No chump, that was certain.

Cassady's brief glimpse of the other flared in his mind. Filling in the blanks, he had the impression of a narrow face, sharp features, dark darting eyes. So, word had gotten back, now Geraci wanted to know the identity and purpose of the big, unkempt man who was trying to locate Bennie. He felt a pleasurable satisfaction: Geraci must be sweating, might even be panicked into making a move that might give him away.

He let the brief satisfaction fade, aware of a troubling in his reasoning. Something he'd missed, had overlooked. He reassembled his thoughts. Yeah, the press had named him as the officer who'd found Skousen's mutilated body; Geraci wouldn't have missed that. Neither would he have missed the reason why he'd followed Lois to the apartment. But would Geraci have spotted him in his present role? Safer to assume so. And if so, why the tail? What did he hope to learn? Did Geraci hope he might lead him to Bennie or Lois? That didn't ring right; Geraci had too many eyes and ears on the street to bother with him. What then? Why the thin man? *Skousen's murderer?*

Christ, Pinto! He knew it! Cassady's scalp tightened as

he viewed the thin man in new perspective. The image of his abrupt move into the dark doorway flooded back. Inexperienced? Hell, no, the thin man had been trying to set him up—had wanted him to spot him. Had he gone back to that doorway to brace him, that would have been it. Exit one traffic sergeant.

He scanned the area carefully. He didn't think there'd be a second tail—the thin man wouldn't have wanted a witness—but he couldn't discard the possibility. Satisfied he wasn't followed, he retreated back along the dim side street.

Flash relived the terror in his mind. When he'd seen Pinto follow the big guy from the bar, he'd had to force himself to tail them from the other side of the street. He didn't know Pinto but he sure knew his reputation. A hit man, Manny once had confided, when Pinto had entered Gino's while they were having pizzas. Since then he'd heard plenty about him. Man, everyone stayed clear of that guy.

Sight of Pinto's abrupt move into a recessed doorway had brought him to a halt. Standing rigidly in the darkness, he was certain the big guy had spotted his tail, was equally certain that if he started toward the doorway he was dead. Just the thought made him sweat anew, fear clotting his throat.

But the big guy hadn't. Instead he'd strolled almost unconcernedly for another couple blocks with Pinto clinging to him like a shadow. Greed battling fear, Flash had forced himself to follow. When the big guy turned down the dark side street, Pinto had darted to the opposite curb before hurrying to the corner. His swift scrutiny completed, he'd whirled back. Terror-stricken, Flash had bolted into the stairwell of a walk-up apartment. His switchblade ready, he'd waited a good ten minutes before he was sure he'd escaped Pinto's sharp eyes.

With the danger past and his second double tequila nearly gone, he sat at the rear of Galliano's on Pedro Street trying to calculate the value of his information, and of that he might learn. Somehow everything was related—the big guy's search, Skousen's murder, Lois' hurried visit to Bennie's, Bennie's frantic flight. The Syndicate wanted Bennie and the hooker; that knowledge was all over the street. Now they wanted the big guy. How much was information about him worth? Plenty. But, Christ, Pinto! He could sell them Bennie. If he tried, would they ask themselves how much he really knew? Flash winced.

He nursed his drink and tried to work it out in his mind. He'd been fighting that battle with himself all day. Would they just pay him, let him walk away? Or . . . Contemplating the "or" made him almost sick. Maybe he could negotiate anonymously by phone. Call some guy like Big Joe Orkie. Everyone knew he was a wheel.

He tested the idea, one he'd had before. Still, he'd have to meet him—or someone—to collect. Suppose that someone turned out to be Pinto? Jesus, a cut throat, that's what he'd get . . . his balls cut off. Yeah, that's how they'd pay him. He didn't want any part of Pinto. That left only the big guy. He brooded about it. Maybe he'd pay.

Flash pictured him again: a good six-one or -two, rugged, unshaven, clothes that could have come from a midnight mission. . . . How in hell could a guy like that pay? Yet he had to be someone if the Syndicate was after him. And if he wanted Bennie bad enough he'd scrape up the dough. How much? Flash debated that. A G maybe. At least he could start from there. Yeah, the big guy would be back, he was certain of that.

A G, a lousy G. Flash contemplated the sum moodily. The Syndicate could throw away that much a hundred times and never miss it. Maybe the phone idea would work. Say he'd heard the rumor, had seen Bennie . . . knew where he was, then see what they offered. Yeah, have someone deliver the information, pick up the dough . . . . Maybe Daisy. Jesus, Daisy would do anything for a couple of bucks. Christ, the fuckin' Syndicate. He felt the sour taste of fear again.

Bennie Worth's hands shook so much he had difficulty controlling the pen. He'd started the letter at least a dozen times, knew he had to finish it. If he wanted to live. But suppose Geraci didn't know about him?

The haunting question came back and he groaned, panicked at the terrible decision facing him. If Geraci didn't know, he'd be cutting his own throat. But Geraci had to know; Frankie sure as hell had spilled his guts. Yeah, Geraci and Frankie. Frankie had been in on it all right, else how would he have known about Geraci?

He stared at the scrawl—nothing but the bald statement that fifteen years ago Angelo Geraci and Frankie Skousen had killed Nancy Cassady during a hold-up, then Geraci had had Skousen killed to keep him from trying to collect the reward by naming Geraci as the killer. What else could he say? Name Lois as the source of his information? That would be worse than no proof at all. But he could say that Geraci was trying to kill him. Yeah, he could say that all right. He added the information with a shaky hand and read it again, deciding he didn't need proof; the cops would take it from there.

Jesus, what was he thinking? The cops wouldn't get the letter unless he was dead! He wanted to reject the whole thing, run and hide, knew he couldn't; without the letter he was damned sure dead. Finally, almost illegibly, he scrawled his name at the bottom of the page. That was the easy part. Now he had to contact Geraci, tell him about the letter . . . what would happen if he was killed.

Just thinking about the task made him giddy with fear.

God, the consequences if Geraci found him! He'd be tortured, forced to reveal where the letter was hidden . . . killed! He hadn't thought of that. There had to be a way, some way. He rubbed his sweaty hands together. But if Geraci knew he couldn't get the letter . . . He seized on the idea. Maybe a lawyer. No, they were all crooks; guys like that would sell him out every time. A bank vault, that would be better. He forced himself to concentrate.

Mr. Geraci, my name is Ben Worth and I know who killed the cop's wife—get him on the phone and give it to him just like that. Tell him what's in the letter . . . say it's in a bank vault with instructions to give it to the cops if he was killed. Geraci sure as hell couldn't crack it from a bank.

He breathed easier, feeling a reprieve. The letter would force Geraci to make damned sure he stayed alive. No one could touch him. No one! Geraci would pass the word fast enough. Geraci might even try to soften him with a bribe. The fantasy was fleeting, not convincing, and when it passed he felt dead inside. The call . . .

Mr. Geraci, my name is Ben Worth. . . . He rehearsed the opening several times, his voice faltering. He couldn't do it; he knew he couldn't. His voice would crack. Besides, he hadn't the faintest idea how to reach Geraci. The knowledge brought a surge of relief. Better to send the message through someone else, a middleman; that would be safest. Someone high, who could reach Geraci. Who?

Orkie . . . Big Joe Orkie. The name came with a rush. Everyone knew Orkie was big in the rackets, and he hung out around Gino's. He'd seen him there several times while he was meeting a source. Cevio, who ran the place, would probably know how to reach him. Cevio knew everyone. Yeah, Orkie. That way he wouldn't have to call Geraci.

He reviewed the plan nervously. Suppose it didn't work? His fears surged back. Better if he got out of town, maybe San Francisco. If he had the money . . . He thought of the reward again. How much would the cop pay for the letter?

Or would the son of a bitch haul him in, work him over, try to force him to testify? That was one thing. And *if* he paid, could Geraci find him in San Francisco? With a sickening feeling he knew Geraci could. Or in Chicago or New York or anywhere else, for that matter. Jesus, it had to be Orkie.

Bennie wiped the sweat away and looked back at the letter, wondering where he could hide it. Finally he slipped it under a corner of the threadbare carpet, then brought out his kit and began making a fix.

"But so apparent, Giuseppe . . ." The Old Man's dark eyes probed Joe Orkie's swarthy face. "The day for such methods is long past."

"Something had to be learned," Orkie said.

"Pinto?"

"I hesitate to say." Orkie watched the dark eyes in the fragile-boned face steadily; it was not good to avert one's gaze when the Don was speaking. *Don*! Orkie had always thought of him as such, even though he'd never heard the Old Man addressed that way. Or by any name or title, when it came to that. But the Sicilian was there, implacable behind the dark eyes. On the first of the several occasions when he'd been summoned to the Old Man's presence, he'd heard him murmur a few words to his escort in the tongue. Did the Old Man know he knew the tongue? Probably.

"It is well to hesitate," the soft voice was saying, "but we know; is that not right, Giuseppe?"

Orkie sighed. "By the way Skousen died, yes."

"What else do you have to tell me?"

"The word is out: find a hooker named Lois Wilson and a pusher named Bennie Worth—Bennie the Needle. The hooker was shacked up with Skousen."

"Who passed the word, Giuseppe?"

"Pinto."

"And Pinto would only act on orders from . . . ?" He watched Orkie expectantly.

"Angelo Geraci, I am certain."

"Ah, Angelo. Do you know the reason for those orders?"

"It was supposedly a matter of money in Bennie's case . . . our money."

"Supposedly?"

"Bennie is a piss ant . . . no part of our business."

"And the woman?"

"She was with the cop who offered the reward when they found Skousen's body."

"And for that there is an order?"

"She was named, yes."

"What do you make of it, Giuseppe?"

"She had information to sell; that had to be it."

"What kind of information?"

"It must have had to do with the reward."

"Of a certainty."

Orkie shifted uncomfortably. "Meaning no disrespect, Sir, I'm puzzled."

"Puzzlement is woven into the grand scheme of life, Giuseppe. And why are you puzzled?"

"The thought just occurred that I might have spoken too soon . . . with regard to Geraci passing the order."

"You have conflict, Giuseppe. Why?"

"The torture-murder. It struck me that Pinto might have been trying to get information to grab the reward . . . was acting on his own."

The Old Man nodded. "It is well to examine all the possibilities."

"I don't like the attention this Skousen thing brought." Looking at the frail face with its deep lines, Orkie thought the Old Man looked more than seventy. All but the eyes. The dark eyes were live things that lived in small caves in the cadaverous body. Bright, penetrating, chill, yet by some controlled power able to suddenly glow softly, gently, when he willed them to do so.

"You are right, Giuseppe. We must know the reason for those strange orders."

"From Pinto?"

"Use your good judgment, Giuseppe."

"Not from Pinto." Orkie accepted the rebuke. "I'll find other sources."

"Ah, then we should soon know. I am grateful you came to me, Giuseppe." He raised a frail hand and Orkie rose. As if by magic his silver-haired escort appeared, waiting while Orkie thanked the Old Man for his audience, then led him downstairs. Each time, on the several occasions when he'd talked personally with the Old Man, it had been a different shabby office; each time the silver-haired man had escorted him to and from the Old Man's presence. Yet the Old Man always was readily available—a matter of a phone number, leaving a recorded message, waiting for a contact, which always came swiftly.

The driver was waiting in the black car by the curb. Like the silver-haired man, he was anonymous, silent. Orkie got into the front seat alongside him and lit a cigarette. *The cop, the hooker, Bennie, Pinto . . .Geraci*—he'd better throw Kopke on it, have him put eyes on them all, find out what was happening. And why. The Old Man expected that.

He watched the silver-haired man retreat into the old building, then the black car leaped ahead.

The Old Man consulted a thin, black notebook, reached for the phone and dialed. Before the third ring a sleepy voice answered. "You recognize the voice, Dom?" the Old Man asked.

"Yes, Sir." The voice at the other end was suddenly alert.

"How long has it been, Dom, three or four years?"

"Closer to three, Sir."

"I am sorry to awaken you at this late hour."

"No trouble, Sir."

"I have need of information . . ." The Old Man asked a few questions, listened to the answers, expressed his thanks and replaced the phone. At the other end, Lieutenant Dom Perrotti of Homicide held the receiver a long moment before replacing it in its cradle.

"Who was that?" his wife asked sleepily.

"Business," Perrotti said, "nothing important."

Dom Perrotti lay awake for a long time, staring into the darkness. He was a good cop and he knew it—a professional with an enviable record, respected by his fellow men. Trusted. Blessed with a good wife, Caterina, and a son, Enrico, a law student at Hastings. Now the voice from the past. The past was like a dark wave at his heels, crashing and thundering to overtake him. How many times had he heard that voice in the last twenty-two years? Tonight made seven; he knew exactly.

His mind drifted back. He'd been just a rookie, less than a year on the force . . . a rookie with problems that terrified him as he patrolled the dark streets at night. *His father's sudden stroke and lingering death . . . his mother's cancer surgery and long medical care before she, too, had died. A mountain of bills—bills he'd felt honor-bound to assume. Caterina had firmly agreed. "We'll get by," she'd said, but he'd known it was hopeless on a rookie's pay. A rookie with a wife and year-old son . . . creditors snapping at his heels.*

Then the "counting house . . ." He felt the stabbing pain of memory. A drab old building in the deep shadows of East Seventh. There, according to whisper, money from the city's bookies flowed in for accounting, hence the name. He recalled his turbulence each time he passed the dark structure while walking his midnight-to-morning beat. Gnawing thoughts that kept at him. *There might be cash there . . . a lot of it. A safe? Christ, he couldn't open a safe. And the Syndicate had protection . . . a whisper but he knew it must be true because officially, in the eyes of the police, the counting house as such didn't exist.*

He'd seized on the whisper to put the thoughts firmly

from his mind, but they persisted: *A safe, yes, but there might be other cash. Maybe only a few hundred . . . but cash.*

He'd been crazy, crazy and stupid. Staring into the darkness he wondered how he'd been so crazy. Only at the time it hadn't seemed crazy. Several times he'd checked the door; not part of the routine, but if anyone noticed him and reported it he could always say the door had looked like it might be open. He'd also checked the alley, the back of the building. Always dark, not even a night light—an undeniable sense of emptiness. Burglar alarms? Undoubtedly. Another sense of relief, and of helplessness. Then, on the fourth or fifth night, he'd found the door unlocked.

Unlocked! Standing in the darkness, he'd felt the wild thudding of his heart. He'd found the door unlocked, had investigated; no one could question that. He'd just look.

He saw himself again as it had been, remembered even the fragments of thought. Chaotic fragments. *Moving in through the darkness . . . Flashlight shielded so that only a thin sliver of light seeped out from between his fingers . . . The big steel safe . . . Might as well try to crack Fort Knox . . . The hurried search of the old, battered desks . . . the one in the small office and . . . the money!*

Perrotti grimaced at the memory; he should have known! He'd scooped it up, hurried outside and closed the door . . . had gotten away from there fast. On another street he'd stopped to inspect the snatch: one hundred dollar bills—twenty of them! Looking at them he swore he'd never try anything like that again. But he could pay his debts—pay them and be free and clear. Besides, it was Syndicate money, wasn't it? Not like stealing from an honest man. Even while he told himself that, a small inner voice shouted "*Thief!*"

The following morning after work, stepping from his car in the driveway, he'd seen the .38 pointed squarely at his gut before a slight, olive-skinned man stepped out from the shrubbery. "*Turn around . . . hands against the car!*"

As Perrotti swung around, he saw a second figure covering him from the shrubbery on the opposite side. A deft hand plucked the .38 from his holster, ran over his body in search of a throwaway gun or knife. Finally the command: *"That car across the street; walk like you're with friends."*

"What about my wife and kid?"

"They're okay. Get moving!"

The car was a black late model Ford sedan, no distinguishable characteristics, no chance to glance at the license plates. A stolid, swarthy figure waited in the driver's seat. Perrotti was directed into the back seat, followed by one of his captors; the other sat in front. Perrotti briefly weighed the odds of trying to wrest the weapon from the slight figure beside him, dismissed them with the knowledge he was dealing with professionals. Christ, how had they caught him? Sickeningly, he knew.

"Where are we going?"

Silence.

"For Christ's sake, I'm a police officer!"

Silence.

He was dead! Perrotti felt a sorrow for his wife and son. But if they'd wanted to kill him, they could have done it easily enough when he'd stepped from the car. One slash with a knife . . . quick and silent. So they weren't ready to kill him. Not yet. The knowledge gave him a faint hope. The driver headed toward midtown, turned onto East Third Street, parked in a yellow loading zone.

"Through that doorway." The man beside him indicated an old building. Perrotti was directed up a narrow, musty stairwell and into a shabby office that contained a scarred desk and several battered straightback chairs. Behind the desk sat a lean man, graying, about fifty.

"Sit down," one of his captors ordered. They positioned themselves behind him as he sat in one of the chairs. Perrotti automatically tabulated more data on the lean figure behind the desk: bushy gray brows, dark probing eyes, long nose thin at the bridge, swarthy skin, no visible scars . . . Latin. A dark tailored suit that must have cost a bundle.

Perrotti had thought of him then as the boss. In later years, after his promotion to lieutenant in Homicide, he'd heard the Syndicate's shadowy head referred to as "the Old Man," and instinctively had coupled the two. By now he felt certain they were one and the same. In his own mind, at least, they were.

"You're Dom Perrotti, age twenty-three, a patrolman . . . a wife, Caterina, same age, and a year-old son, Enrico." The voice was unexpectedly soft, cultured. "And you speak the tongue." The lean figure waited.

"My parents were from the Old Country . . . Licata." Perrotti was surprised at the calmness of his voice; he didn't feel that way at all. "My father was a fisherman."

"Ah, yes, Adamo, and your mother Carlotta . . ." The dark eyes never left his face. Despite his tension, Perrotti had to admit that the other had done his homework. Why? The "why" bothered him.

"We noticed your interest in . . . shall we say . . . the counting house."

"I . . . I needed the money." Perrotti wet his lips.

"Medical bills, I know."

"You left the door unlocked purposely," Perrotti charged, filled with bitterness at how he'd been taken in . . . the price he'd be asked to pay.

The lean man nodded, brought out an envelope, opened it and slid four pictures across the desk. Perrotti still felt sick when he thought of them. *There he was, Dom Perrotti, appearing like a red-hued ghost in the infra-red light . . . gazing at the money on the battered desk . . . scooping it up . . . hurrying from the room.*

"I'm not very smart." Perrotti hid his bitterness. "I have the two thousand."

"So pay your medical bills."

"Come again?" Perrotti stared at him.

"From time to time I might call on you. Not often . . ."

Perrotti shook his head. "That was the first time I ever tried anything like that and it'll be the last. No more, so do your damnedest."

"I know that." The lean man nodded. "That's why you're still alive."

"Then what?"

"No more than information."

Perrotti considered it. "What kind of information?"

"You're scarcely in a bargaining position, Perrotti."

"I know that." He eyed the other steadily. "I won't do a thing that will harm the department."

"I don't anticipate asking that."

Perrotti thought again of his wife, his son, and weighed the proposal; the consequences would rest largely with his conscience. "All right," he said shortly.

"When I phone and say, 'You recognize my voice, Dom . . .' "

"I won't forget . . . ever."

His interrogator gestured and Perrotti rose. Going from the room he contemplated bitterly that the pictures, locked securely in a safe, would forever hold him hostage. He hoped the burden of demand wouldn't prove too great. He got in the car without bothering to look at the building, certain that the other would never see that particular office again.

The drive back had been made in silence. At the curb the man beside him had handed him his .38. Slipping it into his holster, he'd walked to the porch without a backward look.

Now Perrotti felt the thrust of his conscience again. Seven times he'd been called upon to violate his trust—seven times in twenty-two years. Mostly the requested information had struck him as trivial, but two occasions he remembered vividly. Both had involved known Mafia figures who'd bought protection from indictment by becoming police informants; both, within a short time of the Old Man's calls, had been found shot to death, their bodies dumped in squalid alleys. Perrotti had no illusions about the part the information he'd given had played in their executions, but he told himself that such punks were no loss to society; after a while he'd ceased to think about them.

And now . . . Skousen. This time a police officer was involved: Sam Cassady. The questions had been sharp, penetrating—the kind a trained investigator might ask. Perrotti mentally juggled them around, seeking a clue to what the Old Man was after.

Suspects? Pinto's name had been kicked around but no proof—just his reputation as a hit man. Yes, he'd had an alibi of sorts—a card game with a couple of friends; they were taking a hard look at that. *Motive?* The reward—Skousen must have known something; the same for his hooker, Lois Wilson, and a two-bit pusher named Bennie Worth . . . Bennie the Needle. *Any suspicion of an accomplice to the murder?* None. *Cassady?* He'd been tailing the Wilson woman after she'd tried to sell him information about the murder of his wife. *What kind of information?* A name. *Had she offered proof that would tend to verify her claim?* Yes, some information not known to anyone except the killers and the police.

There had been other questions but those had been the key ones. Perrotti had given the answers straight, had to. But what had the Old Man been after? Syndicate involvement? Some lead which would enable him to throw the spotlight elsewhere? Trying to decide whether Pinto had made himself expendable? No, something else.

The reward! His mind leaped back. The Old Man was tying threads together, trying to verify something he suspected. The names of the punks who'd killed Cassady's wife? Skousen had been one, Sam was certain, but the other? Is that who the Old Man was trying to get a line on? If so, why? Why after fifteen years? What interest could he have in punks like that? None at all, unless . . .

Perrotti's nerves sang, taut as banjo strings, and the answer was there. No proof, nothing but that certainty which sprang from a vast reservoir of experience, but it was enough. Skousen's long-ago accomplice . . . He grasped the thread, watched where it led.

"Jesus H. Christ," he whispered. But at least that took Cassady off the hook. Or did it? His mind reeled with the possibilities. If the second killer had risen high enough in the Syndicate, the Old Man could be trying to protect him. How? Holy Mother of Christ, Cassady could damned well be the target.

Dom Perrotti struggled with his conscience and reached a decision: he had to know.

6

"YOU'RE QUIET, SAM." LYING beside him in the darkness, Cindy spoke softly, with feeling. She loved this big man fiercely and knew that love was returned, but tonight, even in the heat of their passion, she'd sensed a part of him lying across a vast gulf, distant and remote.

"Thinking," Cassady said.

"You . . . something new?"

"The names of Nancy's killers."

"How . . .?" She clasped his hand, caught by the reason for his remoteness: he stood near the end of a search which had obsessed him for almost all of his adult years. Near the end . . . Maybe soon the phantoms in his mind would be gone and there would be just the two of them.

"One's dead."

His words brought her back. "And the other?"

"A wheel in the Syndicate."

"Syndicate?"

"Syndicate, Mafia, crime family . . . the people who control the city's gambling, prostitution and narcotics rackets."

She felt a sudden stillness. "Do they . . . know?"

"Know what?"

"That you know?"

He laughed softly. "Don't worry, Cindy, I'm a big boy."

"Do they?" she persisted.

"If they don't, they soon will."

"Sam . . .?" Fear clogged her throat.

"I want that son of a bitch to know." He spoke in a low monotone, his mind far away. "I want him to sweat . . . know I'm on his ass . . . make him panic, expose himself, then I'm going to nail him."

"Sam, you'll get help, won't you? Your friend, Garmont."

"This is my job," he said harshly.

"Sam . . .?" He sensed her terror. "I'll be careful, Cindy; I'm watching my back. For the time being I've moved to a room on the other side of town."

"Why?" she asked tremulously.

"Safer." He turned toward her, trying to phrase his words in some way that would be less frightening to her. "I probably won't see you again until this is over. Just a precaution, Cindy. I don't want anyone following me here . . . nosing around."

"I'm frightened."

"Don't be." He pulled her into his arms and stroked her gently, promising he'd be careful even while knowing how hollow the assurance sounded. It wasn't Geraci he had to worry about so much as guys like Pinto. Killers. The Syndicate probably had a battalion of them.

Corporation presidents and board chairmen—Garmont's words came back. That would be Geraci, secure in his high office. He wouldn't have to fight his own battle; he'd do that by phone, through barked orders. Punks like Pinto would be given the job.

Cassady fumed inwardly. Geraci would probably consider him no more than a nuisance, someone to be brushed away with no more than a second thought. Momentarily he was caught with a sense of helplessness. How did one get at a guy like that? How could he nail him with the proof? Bennie's word would mean nothing; neither would Lois'. Still . . .

He grappled with a forming thought. Geraci had a weakness, a big one, why else had his response been so quick? Why the thin man on his tail? Killing a cop . . . exposing the Syndicate to that kind of a storm—he had to be desperate. There was a chink . . . somewhere. What he'd told Cindy was true: he had to draw Geraci out, panic him into a reckless move. Do that and maybe Geraci would give himself away.

Use your goddamned brain, Cassady told himself. *Don't let that slimy bastard perch in his big office while the scum beneath does the dirty work. Get at him, let him know you're going to grab him by the balls. . . .*

Christ, he'd been going at it bass ackwards, plunging in all brawn and no brains, not thinking of anything but nailing Geraci, and with no clear conception of how he was going to do it. All he'd wanted was Geraci face-to-face, and to hell with judge and jury. Garmont was right: keep thinking that way and he'd get nowhere. So slow down. Think.

What did he know about the man? Damned near nothing. When it came to that, what proof did he have that Geraci was the man? None, except Lois' word. Yet how would she have known such an obscure name so high in the Syndicate? And if she had, why had she picked it when it scared her witless? He'd weighed those questions before, and they brought the same answer: *she knew*. Still, he had to prove it.

He reviewed what he knew about Geraci—discouragingly little. From the financial section of the newspaper files he'd culled a picture of a plump-faced man with a high-arched nose, too thin at the base, bushy brows and thick dark hair; the body appeared below medium height, pudgy. Well fed, Cassady thought. Quite ordinary, yet a close scrutiny of the grainy picture had revealed a sleekness of expression, a suavity, a curious bleakness in the dark eyes. The accompanying story had cited him as president of Southwest Investment Enterprises, which was described as one of the state's leading mortgage investment firms.

That name had struck a chord and he remembered occasional whispers: *racket connections . . . a funnel for laundered money . . . Geraci was the financial brain.* Cop talk, locker room scuttlebutt, but you couldn't hang a man for that. Where did the truth lie? Garmont would know. So would the men in narcotics, vice, the special intelligence unit. The latter would know every twist and turn and dark corner—where the tentacles reached and who held the high seats of power. But knowing and proving were two quite different cats. Gambling, drugs, prostitution, loan-sharking, pornography—the usual keystones. Men who couldn't be touched because the element of proof was lacking; and where not lacking, was helpless against the power of the dollar. Cops on the take, and judges and D.A.'s and men in government from lowly councilmen on up—those were the facts that existed in almost every major city everywhere and he didn't believe his own city was any exception.

And *when* he nailed Geraci? A battery of high-priced lawyers would spring from the earth, hidden wheels would turn, juice would flow. . . . He couldn't recall in his entire career that a powerful figure had paid a penalty commensurate with his crime, even in those few instances when a guilty verdict had been returned. At least not when the crime was murder. Damned if he'd let that happen. But that was a bridge he'd cross later. First he had to dig Geraci out, force him into the sunlight, panic him—make him dig his own goddamned grave. The resolution made him feel better.

He felt Cindy stir against him and wondered, as he so often had, at his good fortune in finding her and what she saw in him. What had he to offer her? A cop's life with all its uncertainties. Punks in stolen cars, drunks behind the wheel, exploding gasoline trucks, and twice in recent months his car had been hit by sniper fire while passing through the Rainbow section—that was security? And if he made it through, what would he have? A half-ass pension. He had to do better than that by her. But how? The "how" baffled him.

Cassady stepped into a phone booth, flipped through the directory, dropped two coins in the slot and dialed. "Southwest Investment . . ." The female voice that answered was young, impersonal, a trifle impatient, as if he'd interrupted some task or other.

"Put me through to Geraci!" He barked the command, sensed her hesitancy and uncertainty. She wasn't used to that type of response.

"Your name, please."

"Look, sister, just stick him on the line!" He pictured her confusion as she tried to decide how to handle the situation. Certainly she knew, or suspected, something of the inner workings of Geraci's empire. Seconds elapsed before she spoke again.

"One moment . . ." He had no doubt but that she'd put the call through; had Geraci been out, she would have said so. And she would have repeated his rude, imperative command. Geraci would be trying to pull his thoughts together, but he'd be forced to respond, if only in an attempt to discover the identity of his caller.

"Yes?" The acknowledgment came suddenly, softly.

"Geraci?"

"Speaking."

"The word's going around that you and Skousen killed Nancy Cassady. . . ."

"Who is this?" Geraci rasped.

" . . . and that you had Skousen killed to silence him."

89

"Who is this?" he demanded again.

"You've had it, Geraci." Cassady replaced the phone and whistled a few notes from *Porgy and Bess*. Geraci hadn't asked, *"Nancy Who?"* or denied the charge; not even a *"You've got the wrong number"* or *"You're crazy, fellow"*—nothing but an urgent and somewhat panicky *"Who is this?"* Had it all been Greek to him he would have damned soon said so; but he hadn't.

Cassady stepped outside and looked up at the twenty-story Crossman Building with its phalanxes of tinted glass. Somewhere up there on the fourteenth floor, in an air-conditioned office, Geraci would be sweating. Cassady experienced the delicious sensation of just having kicked him in the groin.

Earlier he'd consulted the directory, had observed the interior layout of the lobby and the exits from the building. Elevators gave access to an underground garage, as did a stairwell. Gambling that Geraci would use either a cab or a chauffeur-driven car, he stationed himself at a corner which allowed observation of both the main and side pedestrian entrances. He didn't believe he'd have long to wait.

He glanced at his reflection in a window. A stubbly beard sprinkled with gray, untidy dark hair and seedy clothes gave him the appearance of a man close to fifty. He looked as if he belonged on East Fifth rather than among the well-dressed people of the financial district.

If Geraci panicked. . . . He tried to assess the possible consequences. Geraci would damned soon know, or guess, the identity of his caller. His only recourse: kill him! The thin man—Pinto?—would be his instrument. But Geraci was also faced with the necessity of keeping his own role secret, yet his appointed killer would certainly be able to piece the story together. Or had. Skousen plus Cassady plus the reward could add up to but one thing, and the thin man would know it. That was Geraci's problem. But Bennie also had to die . . . and Lois. Both Geraci's problems. If the thin man failed, as Cassady fully intended he would, Geraci would be compelled to dig up a second killer . . . and inevitably the story would spread. Would Geraci risk that? His last option would be to attempt to do the job himself. That was what Cassady wanted, hoped for—the moment he'd face an armed Geraci and for a split second before his death Geraci would know the name of his killer.

Cassady shifted uncomfortably. Was he talking about justice . . . or revenge? Garmont had asked that same question, not too delicately, and it had troubled him ever since. Justice, if there was justice—but if the scales were weighted? Or was that a rationalization to make imperative a more sure form of justice? Why, when he thought of the end of his chase, did he always envision that last split-second confrontation? And the feeling that came with it, heady? The feeling of justice . . . or revenge? When did a cop cease being a cop and become just another animal in the jungle? Yet if Geraci were provably guilty, came at him with a gun . . .

Cassady's mind reeled back to a time when he'd been scarcely more than a rookie on the force. *Driving along East Seventh at night . . . the shot . . . the figure dashing from the liquor store brandishing a gun . . . visible through the open doorway, a second figure sprawled on the floor.*

The scene burned vividly in his mind: his pursuit of the fleeting man, shouting for him to stop; but he hadn't. *His gun sighted squarely between the other's shoulder blades, his finger tight on the trigger . . . letting the barrel drop . . . firing . . . the figure falling, shot through the leg.*

The armed robber had proved to be a hopped-up sixteen-year-old kid. Although the liquor store clerk had been killed, Cassady had thanked God that he'd risked letting the robber escape by going for a leg shot. Another time, following a wild eighty-mile-per-hour chase through midnight streets, the car ahead had swerved out of control, caromed off a parked vehicle, had skidded wildly before coming to a crashing halt against a power pole. As Cassady leaped from his car, the driver had crawled out from behind the wheel, had come up with a revolver blazing. In that instant Cassady had remembered the sixteen-year-old, had tried for another leg shot . . . had been hit in the shoulder and side before he'd reluctantly brought up the barrel, squeezing off a shot which had brought the other down with a shattered collar bone. A hopped-up punk, scarcely fifteen, and again Cassady gave thanks that he hadn't killed him.

But it wouldn't be that way with Geraci; not if he was provably guilty, came at him with a gun. That's what Cassady wanted, wasn't it? Gun in hand, face to face while he shot Geraci down . . . wanted him to live just long enough to know who'd gotten him, and why. No leg shot for that bastard.

Judge, jury . . . and hangman. Cassady shifted uncomfortably. His job was to arrest, not play God. Yet if he nailed Geraci with indisputable proof, his lawyers would plead his exemplary life since, or money would pass under the table; even at worst he'd do minimum time, get a pardon, walk out into the sunlight again, a free man. The Geracis of the world seldom, if ever, paid the bill in full. Too much money, too much power, too much knowledge of where other bodies lay buried. But the son of a bitch wasn't going to beat this one. . . .

What would Garmont think? The uncomfortable feeling surged back. Garmont would despise him if he knew he'd engineered the confrontation. So would the members of the Police Investigation Board, and the D.A. wouldn't be able to push it to the grand jury fast enough. Jesus Christ, what of Cindy and the kids? He agonized over that. But if Geraci came at him with a gun . . .

His attention was diverted as a black Cadillac pulled into a loading zone in front of the main entrance and parked. He automatically noted the license number and model before switching his attention to the driver. A square, swarthy face, thick dark hair combed straight back that gave the impression of a man racing into the wind, a thick neck and wide shoulders that spoke of a strong, blocky body; the hands would be square, powerful—chauffeur and body-guard rolled into one, he guessed. He positioned himself near the right rear of the car so he'd be invisible through the rearview mirrors while he eyed the people coming from the building.

Several minutes later a short man in a neat blue business suit emerged, moving quickly toward the car. Dark, jowly face, high-arched nose, thick lips, pudgy body—undeniably the man in the culled newspaper photo. The face of his enemy! And damned worried, to judge by the haste in which he'd summoned his chauffeur following the phone call. To where was he rushing? What counter-action would he take? A panicky order to the thin man to get on the ball? The engine purred to life and the Cadillac moved into the stream of traffic.

"You haven't seen anything yet," Cassady promised him-self. His thoughts sobered. He still had to find Bennie before that link, too, was erased. Bennie and Lois, he corrected, but Bennie first; he seemed the best bet. Turning back to-ward East Fifth, he pushed his way through the crowd.

He glimpsed the slender figure in the late afternoon.

Perhaps he wouldn't have noticed him if it weren't for the flashy yellow jacket—enough to pull his eyes back. The reflection in the glass was not that of the thin man but of another of about the same height and build. The Syndicate? Sunlight, traffic, pedestrians—not the setting for a kill. Neither was the flashy yellow jacket the kind a killer would wear.

Cassady window-shopped his way slowly, giving the ap-pearance of a man with no particular destination. Pausing at another angled window, he caught the figure more clearly—Chicano, he decided; shoulder-length dark hair, maybe thirty, the look and dress of a ghetto pimp. Definitely not Syndicate. And definitely not one who knew the slightest about shadowing or he'd never be wearing the yellow jacket.

Cassady turned casually. Yellow Jacket swung away, paused near the curb as if studying the traffic before crossing the street. Stance, hesitancy, screamed uncertainty, a man perplexed, indecisive. Cassady turned back, his gaze flicking to the angled windows as he moved on; Yellow Jacket was following. This one had information to sell, privacy in which to sell it.

Or was his judgment wrong? Cassady considered it. Nothing in the book said that a pimp couldn't be a killer, or that a killer couldn't dress like a pimp. The yellow jacket could well be protective coloration. While he didn't believe that, he decided not to take the chance.

Cassady entered a narrow doorway beneath a sign that read *Poppy Rooms & Apts.* Climbing a musty stairwell, he doubled back to a small window that overlooked the street and peered down between the shabby curtains. Yellow Jacket had stationed himself in a doorway across the street, was watching the entrance.

Cassady retreated to the far end of the hall, found a fire escape, clambered out and dropped into an alley. Circling the block, he spotted Yellow Jacket and halted. After a short while the slender Chicano began shifting impatiently and finally moved back along the way he'd come. Definitely not Syndicate, Cassady decided, as he fell in behind him.

The Chicano several times approached men who, in turn, had a searching look. All had shaken their heads and Yellow Jacket had walked away. Cassady envisioned a montage of his contacts: middle-aged men, conservatively dressed, office types, all with searching looks. He concluded that the Chicago was either a homosexual or a pimp, but possibly one with information. Or . . .? Heeding the whisper of caution, he continued to tail him.

In the next block Cassady watched him approach another middle-aged man; this one proved more receptive. Money passed into the Chicano's hand, then he pointed toward the entrance of some nearby walk-up apartments. When the middle-aged man disappeared through the doorway, Yellow Jacket hurriedly left the scene.

A Murphy man! Cassady had to laugh. By the time his victim discovered he'd been gulled, Yellow Jacket would be working his racket blocks away. Cassady had to admire his psychology—victims who looked like they had a few dollars to spend, and who couldn't afford to shout for the police. But he was satisfied, certain he knew his man. The Chicano would keep an ear to the ground, know the street's whispers . . . had reasoned that anyone so anxious to find Bennie would pay for the information. Another Murphy job. He'd been held back only by the fear of being seen talking openly with him. But there was also an outside chance that he did know something. If he did, Yellow Jacket would find him again.

He resumed his search.

Lieutenant Dom Perrotti parked the Delta 88 behind the Empire Bakery, threaded his way across the street and entered Bernardi's Pizza Parlor, taking a booth at the rear. In the late afternoon the place was nearly deserted, which was the way he wanted it. He ordered a beer, then saw Sneaker enter and said, "Make that two."

His narrow shoulders hunched, Sneaker limped to the booth and slid in across from him. Perrotti regarded the ratlike face with its small eyes, a faded brown, the half-open mouth with its rotted teeth, the stubble of gray beard, all in keeping with the crummy clothes that must have come from the Salvation Army. He savored the other's nervousness, underlying currents of fear which manifested themselves by the twitching of the weak jaw. That, too, was the way he wanted it.

When the waiter delivered the drinks and shuffled away, Perrotti leaned forward. "What's the big whisper, Sneaker?"

"Whisper?" Sneaker attempted to look puzzled.

"Cut the shit, I'm in no mood for it."

"I don't know what you mean," Sneaker whined.

"You've been on these goddamned streets for thirty years, Sneaker, except for the years you've been locked away, and you damned well know everything." Perrotti gave him a few seconds to absorb that. "I've never really leaned on you but this time I'm going to, so what's the big whisper?"

"Jesus, Lieutenant . . ."

"Remember Arturo? You heard that whisper and now Arturo is doing ten. You want his people to know who tipped us? They'd cut your fucking throat before the night was out."

"Christ . . ." Sneaker's hand trembled so much his beer slopped over the brim and he hastily removed his hand.

Perrotti leaned back. "Let's have it."

"You mean . . . the Skousen thing?"

"Keep talking, Sneaker."

"I'm dead if it gets out," he whimpered.

"Talk and it won't get out."

"Pinto . . ." Sneaker mouthed the name in a barely audible whisper.

"Old hat."

"Jesus, you know ever'thing I know, honestly."

"You tell me, and you'd better damned well get it right this time."

"The word's out he's lookin' for Skousen's hooker . . . name's Lois."

"Yesterday's whisper."

"And Bennie," Sneaker added hurriedly. "Bennie the Needle—Bennie Worth, I heard his name was."

Perrotti regarded him stoically, letting his fear build. The information so far confirmed what he'd already heard or suspected, but he had a hunch that Sneaker was holding back. Finally he leaned forward again and dropped his voice. "I warned you, Sneaker. Arturo's people will cut off your balls."

"Jesus," Sneaker moaned, "Lemme think."

"You've got five seconds."

"The big guy . . ." he whimpered.

"What big guy?" Perrotti felt a tingle of anticipation.

"He's been askin' questions about Bennie, tryin' to find him."

"Describe him!"

"Jesus, I jes' heard . . ."

"Talk, Sneaker!"

"He's big, maybe six-two or more, a husky bastard. Looks like a bum. He's been askin' all over."

"Get to the point, goddamnit. I'm not going to warn you again."

"He's supposed to be a cop. Someone recognized him."

Cassady! Perrotti leaned back, for a moment forgetting the snitch across from him. Cassady believed Skousen had been one of his wife's killers, and he agreed. But why was Cassady so hot on Bennie? Did he think Bennie had been Skousen's partner? Not Bennie, for Christ's sake; Bennie was a punk, a small-time pusher. Cassady knew better than that. But Bennie knew something; his hurried flight told that. But what? Or what did Cassady think he might know? The identity of Skousen's partner? If he did, and he was right, he was treading a thin, thin line.

He reviewed his own reasoning again. The hooker had gotten the story from Skousen, had teamed up with Bennie to sell Skousen . . . or Skousen's partner. In either event, the partner had gotten to Skousen fast. Through Pinto, he corrected, and Pinto had milked Skousen dry. That much looked fairly firm. Had Cassady found more? Whatever it was, Cassady must think Bennie could tie it down. Tie down what?

A small vein throbbed at Perrotti's temple. How did that fit in with the Old Man's call? Why his concern? Because Pinto had thrown a spotlight on the Syndicate? No, it was something more. The partner . . . *someone high in the Syndicate.* He felt his nerves jump. Jesus Christ Almighty, did Cassady know what he was monkeying with? Perrotti had the sense of a connection almost made, but there was still that small gap, an elusive piece that would complete the fit. Did Sneaker know more?

He brought back his gaze, looked coldly at the snitch, let him squirm a moment before saying, "One last chance, Sneaker."

Sneaker trembled, his face terror-stricken. A thread of saliva ran down from a corner of his mouth. His jaw jerked convulsively before he managed to whisper, "Pinto's supposed to be after him."

"The big guy?"

Sneaker jerked his head in assent.

Perrotti relaxed back against his seat. "Not too bad, was it?" He pushed a crumpled ten-dollar bill across the table, watched the thin, veined hand seize it. "But keep on it; I'll expect more."

"Yeah, sure . . ." Sneaker slid out from the booth and looked worriedly around before he skittered toward the doorway.

Perrotti lit a cigarette and signaled for another beer. Pinto! A goddamned hatchet man, a fucking sadist, but clever enough not to have been caught. Not yet. Not since his early days. Since then he'd learned. Pinto had damned well butchered Skousen. He should have pulled him in, witnesses or no witnesses, but maybe by letting him run . . .

Perrotti assembled the bits and surmises, weaving a pattern. He considered the known facts, the logical ones, the suspected ones, extended them. Behind Pinto was someone far higher, a man who could give a hit order at a time when the Syndicate was trying to tailor itself with a legal mask. That man would be . . .*the second killer*? Logical, but who? Not Big Joe Orkie but Orkie would know, unless . . .

The qualification, popping into his mind, tantalized him. Unless what? Unless Orkie had been sidestepped. Someone very high then. Perrotti breathed more easily. Jarvie? Fifteen years ago Jarvie had still been in New Jersey. Galtner, board chairman of . . .? He shook his head impatiently; Galtner was too damned tall, over six feet. He wanted someone short and . . .

Geraci . . . Angelo Geraci! Perrotti's mind raced, caught with a familiar excitement. Geraci was the right height and age, had been raised in the area, had once been a runner, a bookie. Angelo Geraci, financier, but back then he'd been a tough monkey. Geraci could damned well be his man. Yeah, Geraci . . . no more than a whisper to link his business empire with the Old Man's shadowy world. Yet the link was there, even if the feds looked the other way, professed not to see it. But the police knew—the provable which couldn't be brought to proof because of walls of power, of money. Of politics.

Perrotti considered that coldly. He doubted that Geraci was all that big, but he had to be protected because of the link to the Old Man. Yet Geraci would be of small moment if the welfare of the Syndicate were at stake. Then the question: Was the Old Man trying to protect Geraci . . . or had Geraci acted on his own? If the former, Cassady was dead, dead, dead. And if the latter . . .? Geraci would be cold meat. But Pinto . . .

By the time Perrotti finished his beer, he knew what he had to do. Always the goddamned bottom line, he reflected. Well, he'd bought twenty-two years.

7

CASSADY WASN'T SURPRISED TO see Yellow Jacket slide onto a stool next to him at the small counter cafe where he was having breakfast. He continued reading his newspaper, aware the other was studying him covertly while sipping his coffee.

Finally Yellow Jacket leaned closer. "I hear you're looking for Bennie." His soft whisper held the musical notes of his native Spanish.

Cassady glanced around, his earlier impression of youthfulness vanishing. Yellow Jacket's narrow face mirrored all of forty years. Ghetto years. Pitiless dark eyes, crinkled at the corners, and a ferret nose above thin, bloodless lips gave the appearance of a hunter rat.

"Could be," he acknowledged.

"You've been askin' . . ."

"Here and there." Cassady nodded.

"You a narc?"

"Do I look like one?"

"Doesn't matter." Yellow Jacket attempted a careless shrug. "I can show you where to find him."

"Another Murphy job?"

"Murphy?" Yellow Jacket's flashing smile was false. "A man's gotta make his bread."

"Not at my expense."

"I'm not foolin' you, man."

"What's your name?"

"Why?" The dark eyes were suddenly wary.

"I like to know who I'm doing business with."

"I like that business part." Yellow Jacket hesitated. "Just call me Flash."

"So where's Bennie?"

"That's a money question, man. I don't see any bread."

"You have a price in mind, right?"

"A G, man . . . ten big ones."

"Think I'm gold-plated?"

"You want him bad, I know that."

"Not that bad."

"Bennie's popular, man." The white-toothed smile came again. "A lot of guys want him."

"So why not sell to one of them?"

"Maybe I will."

Cassady smiled. "I've heard rumors that someone in the Syndicate's looking for Bennie."

"Christ, man . . . !" Flash drew back.

"If they want him, you have a gold mine."

"No way, man, I don't fuck with those people."

"Then you haven't a market, right?"

"I know other guys. . . ." Flash sounded unconvincing.

"You know plenty about the street, don't you?"

"Plenty, man."

"Including the names of the guys who want Bennie?"

"Jesus . . ." Flash licked his lips.

"Twenty says you don't." Cassady watched the Chicano struggle with his thoughts, indecision in his face.

Finally Flash leaned closer. "I don't see any green." Cassady brought out his wallet, plucked a twenty-dollar bill from it, returned the wallet and folded the bill into quarters. Flash eyed it uncertainly.

"If the names are phony . . ." Cassady let his tone of voice convey the threat.

"One name, man, just one; that's all I know."

"Just so it's the right one."

"It will be, man, I can guarantee that." Flash struggled with his thoughts again. "His name's Pinto."

Garmont was right, Cassady reflected. He watched the Chicano's face. "First or last name?"

"Just Pinto, that's all I know."

"What does he do for the Syndicate?"

"He's Mr. Big, man, Mr. Big."

"In what way?"

"He sees that guys pay off."

"An enforcer?"

"Something like that."

"What does he look like?"

"Short, thin, a narrow face, maybe forty and real sharp weeds, man. Always wears a black hat with a snapdown brim; that's his trademark." Flash eyed the bill in Cassady's hand. "That's the bundle, man."

Cassady relinquished the bill. "How do you know where Bennie's hiding?"

"I followed him."

"When?"

Flash hestitated. "I saw a chick run out from Skousen's . . . real excited like. He's the guy that got cut. Ya heard?"

"I heard."

"I could tell something had happened and I followed her. Man, she was really taking off."

"You know her?"

"Yeah, by name . . . Lois. She was Skousen's hooker, a real dog, man."

"So where did she run to?"

"To Bennie's . . . the Golden Rooms."

"Keep going."

"She ran out again, real jittery, then took off. Bennie was right on her heels, lugging a suitcase. Man, then I knew something was up and followed him."

"Why him instead of the girl?"

"He's in candy, man . . . got more to lose."

"Guys like that don't stay long in one place," Cassady suggested.

"Man, he's pinned, afraid to move. I check him every day. Doesn't even go out to eat; they feed him there."

"Check him how?"

"A chick, man, she's in the same house . . . turns her tricks there. Daisy. I've known her a long time."

"Daisy? Oh, I might know her. A short blond about forty, right?"

"Nah, dark hair, thin . . . not a day over twenty-five."

"What's the address?"

"Man, that's G talk, like I said."

"Okay, I'll pass." Cassady gestured dismissal.

"A couple of C-notes?" Flash asked anxiously.

"One."

"Now?"

"I don't carry that kind of cash with me."

"When?"

"Maybe tomorrow."

"Here?" Flash insisted.

"Later in the evening, say around seven." Cassady dropped some change on the counter and walked out without a backward look.

Flash toyed with his empty cup as he tried to figure the big guy's angle. Bennie owed him something for sure, and he meant to collect. Well, he couldn't collect until he found Bennie. The thought was satisfying, yet along with it he felt a perturbation—a missing part, a something he didn't know.

His mind went back to the hard, square face beneath the stubble of whiskers, the chill gray eyes. For a brief moment after sliding onto the stool alongside him he'd smelled "cop," but the fear had quickly vanished. He was too crummy for a plainclothes cop, asked the wrong questions for an undercover narc . . . and no goddamned cop would shove him a twenty like that. Not a pusher, not an addict, and he'd had to have really done something to have the Syndicate on his ass. So who was he?

Flash pondered the question uneasily, trying to fit him into a niche. *Big . . . not fat, just big. Looked like a bum but he wasn't, not by the way he'd let loose of the twenty. Soft voice, but those goddamned eyes like gray ice. The Syndicate on his ass and he didn't give a fuck . . . a tough bastard.* Flash shuddered. Not the kind of a guy you'd steer through the wrong doorway.

A Murphy job! It came to him suddenly and his skin crawled. "Another Murphy job," he'd asked. Christ, he'd known . . . must have tailed him. Why? Jesus, had he tailed him to Bennie's hideout?

Flash felt a moment of panic. If so, why the twenty? Because he didn't know. Not yet. Yeah, the big guy still needed him. He breathed easier. But he'd have to watch his steps. At least the big guy stood out like a turd in a punchbowl.

One goddamned C-note. He felt a surge of resentment. Bennie was a gold mine—the big guy had said so himself, then had conned him down to one goddamned C-note. Man, no one conned Flash Gomez and got away with it. He knew a few tricks himself.

How much would the Syndicate pay to know Bennie's hideout? That question had plagued him from the start, but he'd always rejected it, afraid even to think about it. Now he forced himself to dwell on it. Who in the Syndicate? He contemplated it, a shadowy world that went up and up to where even the whispers dwindled and finally died away. Christ, all he knew about it were the whores they shook down, the gambling joints and pushers that paid off . . . a few small fry. Pinto, yeah, everyone knew about Pinto. And Big Joe Orkie.

Geraldo . . . He grasped at the memory. *Geraldi . . . no, Geraci, that was it.* The name had come from somewhere deep in his mind, but where had he heard it? Maybe a rumor, a whisper, but he was certain it had to do with the Syndicate. Someone big, maybe even the top guy. He'd ask around. Get to a guy like that and maybe he could sell the whole package—Bennie and the big guy both. Set the big guy up for them. Yeah, but collect the C-note first.

His fingers trembled as he lit a cigarette. Man, he was onto something really big. The right contact, that was all.

Dom Perrotti watched Cassady leave the cafe. Sitting in the Delta 88, his thoughts were musing. Cassady was kidding himself. For all his old clothes and unshaven face and rumpled hair, the cop was still there, plain to be seen. An air of authority, the way he moved, a watchfulness—those were the hallmarks that Cassady couldn't shake. But would anyone but a cop know that?

Perrotti returned his gaze to the yellow-jacketed figure at the counter. Earlier he'd seen Cassady enter the cafe, had seen the Mexican's hesitancy and careful observation before taking the stool alongside him. *Flash* . . . he'd concentrated briefly before the name came to him. A pimp . . . a Murphy man . . . a one-time graduate from the swarming ranks of young purse snatchers; a graduate, too, of the state's so-called correctional system. Cassady and the pimp . . . and the pimp had information to sell.

How did that tie in with Skousen? Bennie? The hooker? Pinto? He put the threads together again, a damning fabric. Pinto was Angelo Geraci's man; he'd pinned that down with Hendel, in the intelligence unit. Did Cassady know he was one short stop from his own obituary? *Geraci!* Only Geraci was sacrosanct; catch him raping a child at high noon at Seventh and Broadway and the most he'd get would be a ticket for impeding traffic. And the ticket would be quashed. That was a fact of life, of the big goddamned machine that ran things. No one touched the engineman. Geraci wasn't the top but he wasn't far below. How far? One step? Two? *Was* the Old Man protecting him? That was the critical question.

He went back over the Old Man's call again, analyzed his words, his questions, his tone, attempted to sense the attitude behind them. Some of the questions concerned information he should have known. Were they to mask what he'd really been after? *Motive? Suspects? Accomplice? Cassady?* He could forget Cassady; the Old Man had certainly put that one together.

Accomplice . . . the word came like a small pressure against his mind. If he were trying to protect Geraci, he would have known the latter's role . . . the full details, right to a T. Had he simply been trying to determine if Geraci's name had been mentioned? Logical because he certainly knew the intelligence unit would be aware that Pinto would be Geraci's man. Had the other questions been masking devices to cover that one point? Possibly. What then?

Perrotti picked his way patiently through the conversation again, came to the same dead end, then tackled it from the negative: Suppose the Old Man wasn't protecting Geraci? A new ball park. In that view he'd been trying to elicit information—had elicited it. So someone—Geraci?—had been holding back. What if Geraci had acted on his own? God, the twists. But if that guess was right, Geraci would go all out; would have to.

He studied the slim figure at the counter. *Come out, you son of a bitch, lead me on....*

"Somebody knows," Geraci said. Staring at Pinto's narrow, expressionless face, he tried to quell his inner agitation. "The son of a bitch told me the word was out ... said I'd ordered Skousen killed."

"Somebody ...?"

"The cop ... it had to be that goddamned cop."

"So why would he call you? If he knows something, why doesn't he haul you in?" He shook his head. "Because he doesn't know, that's why. If it was the cop."

"It was the cop, all right. I've got a feeling about that bastard in my bones. A goddamned bloodhound. You'd better burn him fast, before he burns us."

"Us?" Pinto cocked a brow.

"Yes, us. You left your trademark all over the place, the way you slaughtered Skousen. You might as well have printed your name on the bastard's chest. That cop will have you right in his sights, and don't think he won't. Why do you think they questioned you?"

"Just checking, Angie. Lucky I was playing cards with the boys."

"That cop still knows."

"Has anything been proved?"

"Don't fool yourself, Pinto. A lot of people know things they can't prove, and that cop knows."

"How was I supposed to make Skousen talk, pat his ass and say, 'Please tell me, Frankie?'"

"You're not thinking, Pinto." Geraci's dark eyes were suddenly cold. "Who else besides the cops would recognize that fancy bit of work of yours?"

"You tell me."

"The Old Man, don't you think he knows? And what else would he think? Why would Pinto butcher a down-on-his-ass skid row punk? That's what he'd think, and you know the first thing he would do? He'd check every angle—Skousen, the hooker, the cop, the reward—then he'd know why you did the butcher job, Pinto. Christ, we're in deep shit."

"It'll get deeper if the cop's knocked off."

Geraci eyed him, fuming while he tried to conceal his inner tumult. Pinto was like a piece of goddamned ice. "Like I said, an accident, or make it look like a punk with a switchblade out for a thrill or a few bucks. That happens everyday. Look at it this way: that cop's down there now, walking the street, asking questions. How long do you think it'll be before he finds something? That bastard's dynamite. So is that hooker . . . that Bennie."

"Not for long," Pinto said imperturbably.

"No more trademarks."

"You're telling me how to do it, Angie?"

Geraci hesitated. "Just do it . . . fast."

"Fast?" Pinto shook his head. "They're not standing down there together, Angie. Bennie and the hooker have crawled back under the woodwork somewhere. If you want it fast, you have to make people talk, and give me the kind of guys who can help wrap the job up. I can't be everywhere at once."

"Then the guys would know."

"They wouldn't know a damned thing; they'd know better than to know."

Geraci drummed his fingers against the desk. Pinto was right; it would take him too long to run down all three by himself, and time was what he didn't have. But, Christ, the danger! He had the feeling of events rushing out of control. No way but to trust Pinto . . . Pinto's judgment. He looked back, sensing that Pinto was enjoying his discomfiture. "Who?" he asked reluctantly.

"Miller and Hein."

"Okay, just do it."

"There's one more complication, Angie."

"Complication?" Geraci felt the sharp edge of fear.

"Have you been talking to anyone else about this?"

"Talking? You think I'm crazy? Why?"

"Some punk has been asking around about you."

"Asking what?" A vein throbbed in Geraci's neck.

"Where he can find you."

"Who is he? Have you checked him out?"

"I just got the word. He's a Mex, a cutout artist; he probably knows Bennie."

"You think Bennie told him?"

"Maybe, or maybe it was the hooker." Pinto shrugged. The cop, the hooker, Bennie . . . now the Chicano. Geraci had the feeling of watching a minute hand sweep toward the zero hour. And he'd committed two more men to Pinto—men who'd damn well figure things out. Before long everyone would know. He should have handled the job himself—years ago. Well, the Chicano should be easy to find.

He shifted his gaze to Pinto's small black eyes. "A guy like that wouldn't be missed."

Pinto nodded, rose languidly, and at the door turned back. "Don't sweat it, Angie." Geraci watched the door close behind him. A snotty bastard, dangerous. A damned sadist, beating up prostitutes, kicking them silly. Jesus, the things he knew about him. Torturing Skousen hadn't been a job; it had been a pure sexual thrill. Bloodless, nerveless, he didn't give a damn what the Old Man might think.

Geraci lit a cigar, his hand trembling. Until the moment he'd told Pinto, he hadn't really thought about the Old Man knowing, but there it was: he had to know. And knowing? He remembered that long-ago day when he'd sat across from him in the shabby office—his denial that he'd ever killed a man, and the Old Man's soft question: "A woman?" He'd admitted it, had to, realizing the Old Man knew all about the murder of Nancy Cassady. And knowing, had chosen

110

him—had raised him to his present position of stature and power. He grasped at the hope. If the Old Man hadn't minded the murder of a woman . . .

He felt the hope slip away, the despair return. This was different, threw a spotlight directly on the Syndicate. The reward, Skousen's butchery, Cassady on the scene—even a cop in Nowhereville could put that one together. And what would the Old Man's first question be? *"Who gave Pinto the order?"* Angelo Geraci, that's who, and the Old Man would know it.

Geraci wiped the perspiration from his brow. He had to get his story together, fast. He imagined himself back in a drab office somewhere, looking into those dark probing eyes—trying to explain. What could he say? *Skousen had seen the reward, was trying to sell him.* The Old Man would certainly understand that. But the torture-murder—a finger pointed directly at the Syndicate! That, he wouldn't forgive. The low profile, that was the thing. No, he couldn't admit any part of it.

He groaned inwardly. The reward, Cassady, the murder done by his man Pinto . . . how could he explain them? He'd have only one chance and he had to make it good. He forced himself to think calmly. A problem like any other, it had to be tackled as such. First he had to extricate himself, divorce himself from Pinto's action. How? Pinto could have done it on his own, had his own reason, that was the line; and the reason had to be logical. A sadistic thrill? No good. Anyone but Skousen maybe, but with the Cassady angle no one would buy that, least of all the Old Man. The reward? That would explain the torture—Pinto's need for information. But how could Pinto have known about Skousen's role? Rumor, whisper, any number of ways.

He imagined himself sitting across from the Old Man again while he examined the logic for flaws. Could he look into those dark eyes and make those statements with certainty? How *could* he be so certain? Christ, he'd nearly missed that one—the kind of a question the Old Man would shoot at him, and rumor and whisper weren't grounds for certainty. He'd heard it? Too weak. An anonymous call! That was it. Someone had called him, tipped him, said that Pinto was shooting for the reward; no one could dispute that. Next was the meeting itself. He fidgeted uneasily. He couldn't wait for the Old Man to summon him; that in itself would cast suspicion on him. He had to initiate it.

Geraci pondered the words he'd use, what he'd say and how he'd say it; and what the Old Man might say. *Why hadn't he called before this?* Another sure question. Easy, he'd just gotten the tip. Contact him now, report the anonymous call, stress his perturbation over the unfavorable publicity the murder was generating; do that and the Old Man would take it from there.

He tested the logic, found it sound. Better, it would take the Old Man a few days to set Pinto up—time enough for Pinto to do the job on Bennie, the hooker, the cop. Yeah, and that Chicano punk. Timing was the key. Do it right and Pinto would wind up in a hot car that had just been reduced to the size of a very small box over in Maynard's junkyard. The Old Man might even instruct him to take care of the job. He'd like that.

Geraci was beginning to relax when he felt the prickling of something he'd missed. Something about Pinto? He searched his mind. Augie Miller and Leo Hein, that was it. He frowned, wondering if he'd been too hasty in agreeing to let Pinto use them. But they wouldn't talk—couldn't if they helped do the job on the cop. Besides, Pinto was too close-mouthed to have mentioned his name. Or was he? Worry nagged at his mind.

The Old Man. Geraci tried to resurrect his image, his voice, his manner. *Silver hair, seamed face, hawkish nose, dark measuring eyes much too alive for the frail body . . . the soft voice. A lift of a skeletal hand was a command.* Now he'd be close to seventy. Or beyond.

Geraci felt a moment of acute discomfort. Who would inherit the Old Man's mantle? His power? What would that mean with regard to him? He sensed, as he so often had, the vast hidden empire of which he was but a small visible face. L.A., Chicago, Detroit, New York, Miami, Las Vegas—wide-spread roots everywhere. A new hand and he could be chopped off like that, never know why or by whom. Or . . .? Momentarily he held his breath. Perhaps he'd be the appointed one. Certainly he'd moved up fast, had proved his worth. It was possible. The Syndicate was a political power, an economic power, a power power, so entrenched that it was represented in all branches of government—federal, state, local—and no one was big enough to fuck with that. He let his thoughts roam, enjoying the moment. A vast plan, a projection, it encompassed the decades to come, hence matters of transition had long since been resolved. Somewhere in that plan was the name Angelo Geraci, a man to be reckoned with.

Geraci forced his mind back to the task confronting him. Tell about the anonymous call, express his concern; that would show he wasn't trying to cover up . . . that he condemned the act. A neat touch. The secret number, the tape recorder, a brief message, and before the night was out he'd find himself in a drab office somewhere, facing the frail figure.

He felt the tremor in his hands, a thudding in his chest. Looking into those sharp, dark eyes . . . he couldn't . . . couldn't carry it off. The Old Man would sense his fear, his evasion, and that would be all for Angelo Geraci. He'd disappear, simply disappear, maybe in the kind of junk car he'd envisioned for Pinto. The mental picture brought a shudder. Another problem, just another problem, and he had to tackle it like any other. The Old Man was the problem; he had to tell him, but how?

Through Big Joe Orkie? He weighed the idea tentatively. It would seem quite natural that he should go through Orkie first, especially since he had no more to go on than an anonymous tip. The Old Man would certainly understand his reluctance to bother him for that. Tell Orkie about the tip, his concern, and it would get back to the Old Man fast enough.

He examined the possible repercussions. Quite likely the Old Man would summon him afterward, want to know all the details firsthand. Well, he could weather that but he'd have to anticipate the questions, be prepared, volunteer no more than was asked. The Skousen killing? He'd gotten the anonymous tip, passed it on; he knew no more than that. The cop? An accident or some punk with a switchblade. No connection. Bennie and the hooker and the Chicano? He could forget them; the Old Man couldn't care less about scum like that. And if the worst came to the worst, he had a bolthole: several fat bank accounts and a current passport. Rome maybe. He could live like a prince and not worry. He pushed the idea back into the holding file; time enough for that if things went sour. Orkie then.

He forced himself to reach for the phone.

Big Joe Orkie scowled at his scattered notes. A hulking man with a slanting brow and bushy black hair, his meaty face masked a mind of unusual perspicacity. It was not a wide-reaching, darting mind, but one which moved with the certainty of a slow freight train toward its goal. Many men had underestimated Orkie; he considered that to his benefit.

The notes—from a personal report and two phone calls—told a lot, yet very little; it was all a matter of interpretation. Not that the Old Man wouldn't know; he *knew* everything. Still, he wanted them straight in his own mind. He placed the notes in sequence. First some Chicano pimp named Flash asking around, trying to find out how he could contact Geraci. Why? Information to sell? Probably. Where Bennie was stashed away? The hooker? But why Geraci? Why would a punk like that think Geraci was in the market? When it came to that, how did he even know about Geraci? Still, the report tied in with the two calls. The same barrel of snakes. Well, he'd hang a handle on the pimp fast enough, make him spill.

Next, Bennie Worth's call—or some guy claiming to be Bennie—babbling about Geraci trying to have him killed. A fucking letter, he'd said. Orkie racked his mind, trying to remember his exact words. *Geraci and Skousen had killed the cop's wife . . . Geraci had had Skousen killed to shut his mouth, now Geraci was trying to have him killed. A bank vault . . . if anything happened to him the cops would get the letter.* That had to be Bennie trying to buy insurance, but what made him believe Geraci was behind the threat? Something he'd gotten from the hooker? If so, he could have passed it to the pimp; that would account for the Chicano's interest.

Then Geraci's call . . .

Orkie leaned back, lit a cigar and ran the sequence over in his mind, trying to tie it in with what he already knew or suspected. Skousen had known who'd killed the cop's wife, or maybe had been in on it. *Had* been, he corrected. He'd spilled to the hooker who in turn had told Bennie, then Bennie and the hooker had tried to sell Skousen to the cop. That tracked. Only Pinto had butchered Skousen first. To protect Skousen's partner? Angelo Geraci? That's how it had looked until he'd gotten Geraci's call.

He frowned. That switched the picture. Now Geraci was dumping the whole thing on Pinto's shoulders. Or was he? Looked at one way, yeah, but looked at another, Angie was simply trying to protect the Syndicate. He remembered back to the early days: a slim, hard, tough kid. Geraci hadn't given a fuck about anything then and that hardness seldom dies. Geraci could have done it all right, but had he?

An anonymous call . . . Pinto making a grab for the reward: that tracked too. That would account for the torture-murder. Pinto would have gotten his damned jollies on that one. Now he was on the hook. Or Angie was. Well, the Old Man would know.

He regarded the notes sourly. He couldn't put all that on tape, no matter how secure it was. Why say anything? *Information on subject*, that would be enough. The Old Man would want to hear the details in person anyway. If Angie was sitting in his big air-conditioned office next week, then he was free and clear. And if not . . .

He reached for the phone.

8

CASSADY CAUGHT THE TAIL in his side mirror shortly after leaving his room. Gray '74 Ford Galaxie . . . four door . . . license plate muddied and unreadable . . . single occupant—his mind automatically tabulated the data. Car clean, free of dents. The plate, he knew, had been muddied deliberately.

He made a few random turns to verify that it was a tail—a lousy one, he reflected. The driver stayed close to the centerline, easily discernible in the mirrors, instead of hugging the blind area to the right. Neither did he vary his distance nor allow another vehicle to get between them. His thin face, not high above the wheel, spoke of a short, slight body. Hair dark.

Pinto? He thought of his morning call. His landlady, her bulging body wrapped in an old brown bathrobe, had tartly reminded him that the phone was *not* to be used that early, and would he *please* remind his friends? He said he would. He'd known then he'd been tailed to his new lodging.

He'd scarcely acknowledged when a voice said, "*A guy named Pinto is out to kill you . . . short, dark, thin.*" The

117

receiver clicked in his ear. Replacing the phone, he committed his impressions to memory: a deep, masculine voice, muffled as if through a handkerchief, and yet . . . He knew that voice; only the face that fitted it eluded his memory. A cop? It had to be, but why the disguise? That made no sense.

Cassady felt a flush of anger. Garmont knew of his search, and who else? Probably a few key men in homicide, narcotics, vice, the special intelligence unit. Was someone dogging his steps, checking his contacts, to see what he'd picked up?

He let his anger die, knowing he was going off half-cocked. Homicide *was* working the case and undoubtedly vice and narcotics were involved; they were doing what they should be doing. Probably someone had spotted him, was giving a friendly tip.

He thought of the call again, the voice, momentarily sensed a coupling of voice and face. When it failed to surface, he returned to what the call had told him. Four things at least: (a) the caller knew he was on Geraci's ass; (b) knew the brevity of information would suffice; (c) he wished him luck; and (d) he *didn't* know that he was already aware of Pinto. That last eliminated anyone acting on orders from Garmont.

New thought: Had the call come from one of Geraci's men? Was Geraci using his own tactics to try to scare him into dropping the case? Cute, but it didn't ring; not with the giving of Pinto's name. The only hard and unassailable fact was that he was under surveillance. Tonight, more carefully, he'd find another room.

He flicked another look at the side mirror. This tail had to be one of Geraci's men. Pinto? Did he hope he might lead him to Bennie? Had his contact with Flash been noted? Or was he looking for an easy way to set him up? Probably all three. Geraci must have the whole street wired, he reflected sourly. Geraci was getting him pegged. Garmont was right:

he was playing an alien game in an alien world. If Flash led him to Bennie, who would follow?

Suddenly he grinned: this was his ball park. Cars and tailing he knew. He visualized the other's consternation if he stopped suddenly, blocked the Galaxie, went back and identified himself and demanded a driver's license . . . threatened him with a ticket for tailgating. Tempting, but not the way.

He stepped up his speed, straddled the two right-hand lanes to prevent cars behind from passing, watched the Ford creep closer, then braked to a sudden stop. Through the rearview mirror he saw the Ford screech to a halt a yard or two behind him, the driver's lips twist in a curse.

Cassady leaned forward as if to scan the stores while watching the mirror from the corners of his eyes. *Slender, dark curly hair, boyish face with heavy pouting lips, a sharply receding chin . . . maybe thirty.* He pulled another picture from deep in his mind, compared the two. *Not Pinto!* They were about the same height and build but the contours of his face were different. This face had an unfinished look—half man, half boy—and with something curiously feminine about it.

Pretty Boy—he filed the tag in his mind. Pretty Boy would be easily remembered. *Brown jacket, a tan sports shirt . . .* His scrutiny completed, he moved ahead. At the next intersection the Ford wheeled around a corner and vanished from sight. He added a mental note: a lousy tail, but smart enough to know he'd been made.

Cassady eyed the mirrors while making several random turns. Satisfied there wasn't a second tail, he continued on to midtown, entered a parking garage and found a slot on the fifth level. For a moment he sat, putting his own situation into perspective. Find Bennie: that was priority one. Locating him through Daisy was his best bet. Watch his back. Keep Geraci off balance. Lois? As of this morning she hadn't returned to the motel, now he was certain she wouldn't. She'd be in another cheap room, hooking on the side streets to feed the beast. How long would she last? Or had she already been found? Disquieting, that, but nothing he could do about it.

He glanced briefly in the mirror; the face that confronted him was that of an unshaven bum. At least he didn't smell. But the eyes gave him away: slate-gray, hard, watchful. A cop's eyes. No way to change that. Patting the .38 in the shoulder holster under his loose jacket, he stepped from the car and headed toward the elevator.

At the intersection of Broadway and East Fifth he stopped in a doorway to scan the faces behind him. Businessmen, shoppers, loiterers—no sign of a tail but he'd have one shortly; of that he had no doubt.

He moved slowly along skid row, absorbing the sounds and sights, the people, sensing the feel of life around him. A hot sun beat down; acrid smog and a stinging in the eyes gave a foretaste of the summer to come. Hungover drunks, panhandlers, a few early hookers—and in a room somewhere, Bennie. If Flash checked him every day he'd be nearby. Someone would know; someone always knew. Daisy was the best bet. Near the Golden Rooms he began his search, this time in the southwest quadrant.

A TD car wheeled past and he recognized Ed Durke, a grizzled traffic patrolman who now had less than a year to go before retirement. Sight of the black-and-white cruiser brought a touch of nostalgia. It would be good to get back into harness again. His eyes targeted a building and he moved toward it.

The faded yellow sign read *Blazer Rooms*. Below, at the narrow doorway, a woman waited. Tall, thin, a chemical blonde with a hard painted face, she wore a yellow blouse and black skirt, both on the shabby side. Cassady approached her and gestured casually. "Hi, I'm looking for Daisy."

"Daisy? That's a new approach." She sized him up, her smile brittle. "Maybe I could help you."

"She's my sister . . . ran away from her husband. I heard she was down here. Slender, dark hair, twenty-five . . ."

She shook her head. "Sure you wouldn't like a little relaxation? I have a room upstairs."

"Maybe next time." He started to move away, then wheeled back. "Would you happen to know Lois . . . Lois Wilson, or Bennie?"

"You're full of questions, aren't you?" She eyed him suspiciously.

"Friends I haven't seen for a long time," he explained. "I've been away."

"That happens." She smiled knowingly. "I can't place the names but if I hear anything . . ."

"I'll check back."

"Upstairs, ask for Edna."

"Thanks." He moved away. Near the end of the block he entered another narrow doorway, ascended a musty stairwell and rapped sharply at the first door at the top. The sound of movement came from inside before it was opened. Confronting him was a short, squat, dark-eyed man of about forty. A dirty blue shirt open at the collar revealed a tangled mass of black hair.

"Sorry to bother you," Cassady said. "I'm looking for Daisy."

"No Daisy here." Dark eyes raked him suspiciously.

"How about the other room?" Cassady gestured.

"You've got the wrong place."

"Know a Lois . . . or Bennie?"

"No!" The squat man slammed the door. Cassady returned outside. From time to time he paused casually to scan the faces behind him. Although he detected no sign of a tail, he had the prickly sensation of being watched . . . followed. But wasn't that what he'd wanted, for Geraci to know he

121

was on his ass? Now Geraci knew. He had taken the first step through Pinto, and Pinto was a killer. So, probably, was the tail he'd spotted earlier. Two men at least, and how many more?

He considered that with the carefulness of a man whose life hung in the balance. Pinto would be the number one man, the others, backups. But no car roaring through the sunlit streets, no blazing guns. Not even the Syndicate could afford to dust a cop that way. Pinto was a pro and would plan his kill accordingly. A gun with a silencer, a place with no witnesses . . . preferably at night. He'd be safe by day, just so he kept his eyes peeled. And the tail was another plus sign: someone was getting panicky. He grinned to himself. Time to panic Geraci again.

He entered a drugstore, found a pay phone, dropped two coins in the slot and dialed. "Southwest Investment . . ." The female voice that answered was the same one as before.

"Stick Geraci on the line," he barked.

"One moment . . ." This time there were no questions, no hesitancy. He pictured the secretary, nervous, hurriedly passing the message: *That same man again . . .* As the seconds drew out to nearly a minute, he imagined Geraci fumbling with his thoughts, trying to formulate his questions.

"Yes . . .?" The soft acknowledgment finally came.

"The word's going around that you've ordered Pinto to kill Bennie Worth and Lois, Skousen's hooker."

"Who is this?" The soft voice erupted into a snarl in which Cassady discerned the overtones of fear.

"They say you're trying to hide Nancy Cassady's murder."

"Who is this?" Geraci demanded again.

"You remember, the woman you and Skousen shot." Cassady replaced the phone and went outside, gazing at the passing faces. If that didn't bring a fast reaction, nothing would. Just his answers had shouted his guilt. Proof? No, but that would come; Geraci might even hand it to him on a silver platter.

Near the end of the block he entered another doorway.

Geraci's hands trembled. Despite the air-conditioning, trickles of sweat coursed down to his collar. It had to be that goddamned cop, and he knew! Pinto had gotten to Skousen too late. How much did he know? He couldn't know more than what Skousen might have blabbed, and even that would have come secondhand. The word of a dead man! No proof at all. Cassady was trying to panic him, force him into some damning admission, probably was taping the calls. If so, he'd learned nothing.

His tension ebbing, he lit a cigar and sat back to review the two calls. No threats, just flat statements. Wait! *"You've had it, Geraci."* He'd closed with that the first time and that damned well was a threat. *Revenge!* The insight crashed in his mind.

Geraci felt a moment of absolute stillness. Had Cassady been making an official investigation (*How could he, a god-damned ticket pusher*) and had picked up an accusation by Skousen, he would have passed it along. In that event the homicide dicks would already have questioned him, even though politely. But they hadn't. Cassady was acting on his own . . . wanted revenge.

Geraci breathed easier. Cassady, alone, was dead meat. He must be stupid. Not a cop, really, just a traffic jockey. But how had he known about Pinto? That puzzled him. Pinto must have been carrying a sign on his back. He swore softly. A simple job and what was Pinto doing about it? Nothing. Nothing but alerting the whole damned town. Pretty soon everyone would know the whole damned story, or guess it, then if the cop was murdered . . .

Geraci tried to discipline his thoughts. No reason to worry. One goddamned cop with some half-assed story from a now dead junkie, and gotten secondhand, at that. But he had to be stopped, and fast. The whole thing would have blown over if it hadn't been for Pinto's fancy knife-work.

He thought of his call to Orkie. Had it been a mistake? The nagging worry came again. He tried to place himself in Big Joe Orkie's mind. Orkie wouldn't condemn him, even if he knew the truth . . . unless it threatened the Syndicate. That was the fucking kicker, and that's exactly what Pinto had done—put the Syndicate center stage. Orkie would be digging, and anything he found would go right to the Old Man.

Geraci fretted, trying to escape the trapped feeling. He had to know what Orkie knew, how much he knew. Without that, he couldn't plug the holes. And Orkie, because the Syndicate was involved, wouldn't give him the time of day. Could he get past Orkie, reach someone close to him? Who? There were always guys who were ambitious, who had the guts to back up that ambition.

Kopke . . . Mark Kopke. He pulled Kopke's image into his mind: tall, husky, a hatchet-faced man, eyes like a snake. Kopke had pulled himself up from the slums, beating a murder rap in the process, now was Orkie's chief enforcer. That took guts, ambition, and he'd be intelligent enough to know he'd reached dead end. He could be slapping whores around and beating guys over the head till he died of old age, or with a knife between the shoulder blades. No future in that.

How ambitious was he? Ambitious enough to go for Pinto's job? That would be a big step up—one he could sweeten with a nice bonus. Kopke would grab at that. He had to get rid of Pinto anyway . . . after he killed the cop. And Bennie and the hooker.

He considered the idea carefully, weighing risk against gain. Kopke was probably involved already, digging up information for Orkie, was probably on top of everything that came Orkie's way. If Kopke was half as smart as he thought he was, he'd damned soon figure out the rest of it; but he couldn't talk. Neither could anything be proved after the cop and Bennie and the hooker were dead. And Pinto.

Could he risk propositioning Kopke? How strong were his ties with Orkie? Or was Big Joe Orkie just another impediment on his way to the top? Geraci fumed at the decision facing him. Risk versus gain, like any financial problem, and he'd untangled thousands of them. This was the same, only he had no choice. It was a matter of how to approach Kopke.

He smiled suddenly as the solution came. Impress on Kopke that absolutely no one else was to know about the job, not even Orkie—say that was straight from the Old Man. Tell him the Old Man saw him as a comer, had named him to clean up the mess, then Kopke wouldn't dare peep to anyone. He'd leap at the chance, would have to. That would make the risk minimal.

Geraci stared at his pudgy hands. If everything else failed, he'd do the job himself.

No Daisy in the Maple Apartments, no Daisy in the Greenwood Hotel, no Daisy in the Lilac Rooms, and the one Daisy he'd found had been ready, willing and able, but was plump, blonde, all of forty-five. The seedy young girl waiting by the newsstand didn't know a Daisy; neither did the hooker who was waiting to catch the men as they came out of a porn movie. Although Cassady had to give her high marks in psychology, her ability to offer information was zero. Or so she'd tried to make him believe, but something in her face had told him otherwise.

He had stopped at the Imperial Pool Hall off Fifth for a sandwich. Paying for a wrapped ham and a bottle of Schlitz at the counter, he carried them to the nearest booth and wearily sat down. The place was empty except for two sailors playing and the manager, he noted. After a few bites, he pushed the rancid sandwich aside and drank deep of the cold beer while brooding over his progress. He'd talked to pimps, prostitutes, bartenders, cab drivers, dozens of people—all close-mouthed, suspicious. None of them had ever heard of Daisy or Lois or Bennie—almost, he thought, as if a blanket of silence had been laid over the entire area. Was that possible? He was beginning to believe so.

He finished his beer, flexed his aching feet and lit a cigarette. No Daisy, no Daisy, no Daisy—the words kept pounding in his mind like a metronome. Recalling the shack area he had passed through with its garbage-filled alleys and young girls who whispered obscenities from grimy windows, he decided the bloody highways were a joy by comparison. Damned if he'd ever cover a beat like this. A couple of years and a cop would be as twisted as the rest of them—would have to be to survive.

His only lead had come from a young-old black girl waiting in a doorway, dark eyes inviting. Slim fingers had plucked the ten from his hand as a large black figure loomed in the doorway behind her. The bill had changed hands again. "We had coffee together a few times—a small cafe near 13th and Imperial." She had pointed, then darted around the black man and vanished into the hallway.

A few blocks and he'd be back at his starting point. Nine hours to cover a single quadrant hit-and-miss, and all he had learned was that a Daisy who might-or-might not be the right one might-or-might-not live near 13th and Imperial. That is, if she existed other than in the black girl's mind.

He glanced wearily at his watch—nearly six—and hesitated. A possibility, but damned tenuous, and where near 13th and Imperial? He'd be hours, and he couldn't afford to miss Flash. He'd better get going. The Chicano was still the best bet.

He spotted the woman as she stepped out from a doorway: blonde, tall, thin, wearing a yellow blouse and black skirt. His eyes flicked up to the faded sign that read *Blazer Rooms* and he recalled he'd come full circle . . . back to Edna.

As he started toward her, she saw him. Her mouth fell

open and the hard, brittle look vanished, leaving her with a foolish, frightened expression. Abruptly she spun back toward the doorway.

"Hold it!" He hurried after her, heard her footsteps clattering up the stairwell as he entered the building. "Edna, wait . . .!"

She swung around and looked down at him. "Go away, please. I don't want to talk to you!"

"Who reached you?" He moved up a few steps.

"Go away," she cried. "Think I want to get my throat cut? Just go away." She ran up the last few steps and a moment later he heard a door slam. So, he'd had a tail. Returning outside, he gazed at the passing faces. Probably everyone he'd questioned had been questioned in turn by one of Geraci's men. One? It would have taken a team, two or three men at least. He laughed to himself; Geraci was panicking.

Almost as quickly he sobered again, then cursed silently. The meeting with Flash was out; he couldn't risk leading them to him. If he did, exit Flash. The Chicano wouldn't last ten minutes if they thought he was peddling information to him. And if he didn't make the contact? Flash would probably check with Daisy to make certain Benny was staying put. Cassady smiled, congratulating himself that he was getting into the swing; he was a pretty good tail himself. Deciding he might need wheels, he started back toward the parking space.

The sense of being tailed pricked at his subconscious. Moving through the evening crowds, he detected nothing suspicious yet the sense of being under surveillance persisted. No amateur this time; the guy was damned good. But this was Pinto's jungle; for all practical purposes he was in Pinto's backyard. Before entering the parking garage he studied the street again. Shoppers, pedestrians, loiterers . . .

It felt good to be back behind the wheel. Safe. Secure. His car, traffic . . . that was his environment. Engine sounds, the blare of horns and squealing brakes fed him data that he knew and understood; each was a message that brought him a picture. And no tail, however wary, would long remain undiscovered.

On Broadway he spotted the dark green sedan, this time a Dodge four-door, vintage '75. While several cars back, the driver had made a burst of speed to close the gap, then had pulled in behind him. A useless maneuver in the heavy traffic, unless . . .

Two pictures came together in Cassady's mind: a green Dodge sedan with two occupants parked at the opposite curb as he'd swung off the ramp from the garage, now a green Dodge sedan with two occupants behind him. The same one?

He watched the side mirror in the gathering dusk. The driver was slender, had dark curly hair, a receding chin. *Pretty Boy!* No mistake. Pretty Boy had been put onto his tail again; that suggested a pretty fair communication system. But he still clung to the centerline and crowded close, hadn't learned.

A stop signal gave him a chance to observe his companion, whose head towered a good six inches above that of Pretty Boy. *Thick dark hair, wide cheekbones, a gaunt face, long chin . . . big shoulders that suggested a powerful body, fortyish.* Cassady tagged him as "Ape."

He pulled into a taxi stand and parked, noting the license number as the Dodge slipped past. Both men kept their faces studiously averted. Cassady pulled back into traffic, turned at random until he was certain there wasn't a second tail, then headed toward East Fifth.

He cruised slowly past Al's Cafe, where he was supposed to meet the Chicano, eyeing the faces and parked cars. No gray Galaxie. No green Dodge. The usual loiterers, passersby. Circling the block, he found a parking slot about fifty yards from the cafe, glanced at his watch and settled down to wait. Flash should be along at any moment.

Flash was vexed, resentful, unhappy. Caught by the vision of big money, lots of it, he'd started making inquiries about Geraci as soon as he'd left the big guy at Al's Cafe. Geraci, he was sure of the name now; the more he ran it through his mind, the surer he was. But no one knew him!

Ponti the collector had never heard of him. Neither had Jackson the pimp, nor Carlie, who made book at Denny's newsstand. He'd tried them first because he considered them authorities on the street. Jeez, they'd been around for a thousand years, knew everyone and everything about everyone. Except Geraci. Or else they were too damned scared to talk; so was everyone else. That was it, he felt sure.

He'd started again in the morning, concentrating on cathouse madams and bookies and cardroom operators on the basis they were all paying off to the Syndicate, but the story was the same: *"Who's Geraci?"* or *"Never heard of him"* and, a few times, *"Whatcha got in mind?"* He wasn't about to answer that last one or they'd want a cut, but they knew; he was more certain than ever. If they were that close-mouthed, Geraci had to be big, damned big. As Geraci's stature kept growing in his mind, he kept escalating the payoff.

At noon, from sheer necessity, he quit for a couple of hours to hustle a mark, then visions of the payoff got him started again.

Manny was just dusting off a chump when Flash entered the pool hall. He watched Manny pocket a couple of bills, admiring his adroitness. Small pale eyes in a moon-shaped face, earlobes that looked like they might flap in a wind and incongruously long arms set on a short frame gave the impression that he'd been built of mismatched pieces.

Flash waited until the chump had left before approaching him. "Howya makin' out?"

"Bacon money," Manny said. "Whatcha got in mind?"

"Know where I can locate a guy named Geraci?"

"Geraci? You mean Angelo Geraci? Jesus . . . !"

"I guess that's the first name." Flash felt a surge of elation.

"Jesus," Manny said again. He drew him to one side and dropped his voice. "Whatever ya got in mind, cool it."

"Why?" The warning bothered him.

"Don't even mention the guy." Manny was obstinate. "I'm warnin' you because we're friends." Yeah, they were friends, all right. He used to steer the stray chicks to Manny's whorehouse in the days when Manny was riding high, and Manny always paid him on the nose. A lot of times they'd split a bottle together and Manny would always cut him in when he got a new chick with something special on the ball. Manny really had it made, paying them off with the needle and just enough chicken feed to let them get by, then something had happened and Manny was out on his ass. Now he was forced to make his bread the way he'd started—hustling the chumps with an educated cue stick. Manny had never told him what the trouble was but he knew it had to do with the Syndicate. Yeah, those bastards got you going and coming.

He tried a new tack. "I got information he wants."

"Ya got nothin', I'm warnin' ya."

"I could cut you in."

"Think I'm nuts? I don't even want to hear the name." Manny chalked his cue stick and moved away. Jesus, Manny giving him the brush-off. Flash went outside and lit a cigarette while trying to decide what to do. Manny's warning shook him but at least he knew there was a Geraci. Angelo Geraci, and he had to be pretty big to scare a guy like Manny. But Manny was dumb, wasn't thinking it through. Why would Geraci get sore if someone told him what he wanted to know? That didn't make sense. With the Syndicate so hot to grab Bennie and Lois and siccing Pinto on the big guy, the information must be worth a bundle. Fuck Manny, he'd find Geraci on his own.

Despite his resolve, he felt a sick fear. He had to be damned careful, do his bargaining on the phone. Yeah, and

130

deliver the information and collect through a third party, then to Vegas or 'Frisco till things cooled off. If a guy was big enough he could do anything. Wasn't that how guys like Geraci made it to the top?

Stick with the whores, he decided. Not the ones in the houses because they were too close to the Syndicate, always under the eye. The ones on the street were different. Because they had to pay a fixed fee every week, they really had to scrounge. They got around, played the bars, the porn shows, the sidewalks . . . were always listening, figuring the angles. If anyone knew where Geraci hung out or could be reached, one of them would; it was the kind of thing some of the punks lower down might throw around in bed while trying to build themselves up.

The first few hours were discouraging. He'd tried all the girls he knew and a lot he didn't. Although they'd all denied knowing the name, a couple of them had shown enough fright to keep his own fear bubbling.

In the late afternoon he encountered Bernie, a male hustler who played the porn shows. A few years ago, in his early twenties, he'd been a striking figure—shoulder-length blond hair, a handsome face, lively blue eyes. Now his clothes were shabby, the blond hair stringy and unkempt, the blue eyes bloodshot in a gaunt, wasted face. Bernie was on the needle.

"Man, you're looking for a cut throat," Bernie said, when he put the question to him.

"It's plenty safe," Flash argued. "I've got info the guy wants."

"Never heard the name." Bernie turned and walked rapidly away.

"Prick," Flash muttered. He glanced at his watch. Less than half an hour before he was supposed to meet the big guy. He couldn't afford not to, couldn't afford the chance the big guy might find Bennie on his own. Jesus, he had to stall him until he found Geraci, but how?

He was heading toward Al's Cafe when he spotted a thin

woman dressed in a blue blouse and tan skirt. His gaze, sweeping past her, triggered something in his mind and he jerked his eyes back. *Skousen's hooker . . . Lois!* Startled, he halted abruptly, then smirked. Man, she was running on junk time, floating, walking in a goddamned trance . . . had just come from the candy man. Right now she didn't give a fuck about guys like Pinto or Geraci. Jesus, the whole Syndicate looking for her, now he had her!

He glanced at his watch again; the big guy would wait. Falling into step behind her, he calculated the added payoff. Now he really had something to sell, both Lois and Bennie. Play it right and he could sell Bennie twice, to both the Syndicate and the big guy. He was figuring how he might handle it when she entered a doorway that led to some rooms above a Chinese restaurant. He debated quickly. She'd stay put through the night . . . float dreamlessly through the long dark hours until she woke in the morning, her body screaming, then she'd have to hit the street again to make her monkey food. But before then . . .

"Yeah . . ." Caught by a new idea, he breathed the word softly. He didn't need Geraci. Both Pinto and Orkie damned well knew him, probably worked right under him. Anything he told them would go right to Geraci. He could work the deal through either of them. *Either of them?* No, Pinto was out; that son of a bitch might cut his throat without a second thought. Orkie then. Big Joe Orkie. He contemplated that. Orkie had to be tough or he wouldn't be where he was. Tough, yeah, but not a knife artist. Not like Pinto. More like a boss, he'd heard. And if he set it up by phone . . .

He smiled, pleased with himself. They wanted all three of them, didn't they? Sure, they had a tail on the big guy but they hadn't been able to get him where they could do the job on him. That's where Flash Gomez came in. Set the big guy up for them! Man, he'd be in clover.

The big guy was the problem. He had to stall him tonight, figure some way to set him up. Returning toward the cafe, he discarded ideas almost as quickly as they came. Everything had to be handled by phone and he'd use Daisy to collect. That way, if there was any rough stuff, he'd be out of it. Still, if they wanted all three of them, they couldn't afford any rough stuff; not till they had all three.

All three? Christ, he had it! Let Orkie know what he had, what he could deliver, and let him know there'd be no delivery till the price was right; nail that down first. Then sell them one at a time—his margin of safety. Lois first, before she was picked up, and next the big guy. *Then vanish!* Collect on the first two, then while they were waiting for him to sell Bennie, he'd be on his way to Vegas or 'Frisco. Yeah, he'd lose a little that way but at least he wouldn't wind up with a cut throat.

The big guy, that was the problem; he had to stall him. He slowed his step to give himself time to think. He had to let him know that tonight was impossible but tomorrow was a cinch. How? The guy was no pigeon, that was for sure. He still got funny feelings about him . . . those goddamned cold gray eyes.

The idea came so suddenly, he halted in mid-stride, caught with a familiar excitement. That was it! Say Daisy had just called, said that some slob in one of the other rooms had cut a chick with a knife, now a couple of cops were staked out there waiting for him to come back. Yeah, the big guy sure wouldn't want to go there with a couple of cops waiting. Then he could offer to take him there the next day, after things quieted down.

Timing, everything depended on timing. Contact Orkie and offer to set the big guy up for him. No, offer to sell all three first; that would really grab him. But would the bastard pay? He'd probably figure it as some kind of a con game. Or maybe he'd refuse to pay until after delivery; that was more likely.

Flash contemplated that moodily. If the worst came to the worst, he'd have to give him Lois on trust; that ought to convince him that it wasn't a con. Orkie couldn't afford not to go for that. Give him Lois, have Daisy collect, then hold off on the big guy until he agreed to pay in advance . . . or maybe settle for half down and half after they got him. Orkie would still have to pay if he wanted Bennie. In advance? Why not? If he paid for the big guy in advance, or even half, why wouldn't he do the same for Bennie? Man, a triple payment! Flash felt the excitement of a sweet promise to come.

He tested the plan. Yeah, it tracked. As soon as Daisy collected on Lois he'd set the big guy up where they could nail him, only it couldn't be at Bennie's; he had to keep Bennie safe for the third offer—his escape margin. If Orkie paid in advance, so much the better. Manny's apartment? He snickered, caught with the delicious feeling of revenge. That would damned well fix Manny for buttoning his lip to a friend.

Could he trust Daisy? He sensed a momentary perturbation. He'd told her he knew Bennie was hiding out because some punks he'd ripped off were after him, and that there might be some money in it for them. Just a matter of finding out how much the punks would pay. She'd bought that without question, but had insisted on a split for keeping an eye on Bennie, explaining she'd have to share with Mae Hammond, who ran the place. Yeah, he knew about that setup. No trouble there, but how much did he have to tell her to get her to do the collecting? That was the sticker. He kicked a few ideas around restlessly. He didn't have to tell the old dyke anything, just Daisy. Christ, even a hint that the Syndicate was involved and she'd leave town.

He swore luridly. Just when he figured he had it, something else always cropped up. But why give her a name? Just say the punks were offering five C-notes for Bennie; tell her where to meet them. She'd button her lip to the old dyke and go for that one fast. He smirked. By the time she found that half of nothing was nothing, he'd be on his way.

Flash arrived at the cafe ten minutes late. A glance through the window told him the big guy hadn't arrived yet. He scanned the street before he lit a cigarette. The big guy would come.

He was visualizing how he'd live it up when he sensed someone at his side and turned. The dark eyes staring down at him were cold and hard. Then he sensed someone at his other side.

9

Relaxed against the car seat, Cassady scanned the street in the vicinity of the cafe. With the onset of darkness the tempo of life was picking up, its beat fast and discordant. People hurrying, jostling, loitering, their faces multi-hued in the glare of flashing neons. The night, warm and muggy, was sharp with the acrid tang of smog. From somewhere came the raucous beat of a juke box. Whoever had dropped a coin in it had been gypped.

He watched a splotched quarter moon rise above the dismal buildings, marveling that men had walked on it. *That* and *this*—the gulf that separated the two was immeasurable. His eyes roved. An old crone investigating a trash barrel; two elderly men conversing under a street lamp, their heads close together; two young boys threading past, talking excitedly. A thin ferret-faced man wearing a dark turtleneck sweater under a loose jacket sauntered slowly toward him, casting a quick look inside each car he passed. Cassady watched him narrowly, sizing him up for a sneak thief. Their eyes met briefly through the windshield before the ferret-faced man passed.

He scanned the cars parked along the opposite curb again, scrunching around in his seat to see those behind him. All empty except the guy in the gray Delta 88, who'd been there when he'd arrived. Turtleneck was darting across the street. No suspicious faces behind him that he could see.

His inspection completed, he turned back, flicked his gaze over the crowd. Two sailors, a woman between them, entered a doorway just past the cafe. An old man paused to take a drink out of a bottle in a brown paper bag, then walked on, his gait unsteady. A teen-age girl sauntered past, her thin face a mask of make-up. Winos, hustlers, sharpies, derelicts—the street seemed less alien now. Another kind of highway, but one where the pulse was slow.

His eyes caught a figure threading through the crowd and he sat straighter. *Flash!* The Chicano had discarded the yellow jacket in favor of a checked blazer, and now wore dark slacks. From the corner of his eye Cassady noticed a tan Chevy moving slowly on the opposite side of the street. When it stopped, double-parked, he turned his attention to it. A driver . . . two figures in the rear seat. The man behind the wheel struck him as slender, with untidy dark hair. Not Pretty Boy. The horns of the cars behind blared angrily and the Chevy moved slowly ahead.

He switched his gaze back to Flash. The Chicano stopped in front of the cafe, glanced through the window, then looked around briefly and lit a cigarette, his movements restless, nervous.

Cassady became aware of the tan Chevy gliding past again, this time from the direction in which it had come. He watched it, tense and uneasy, automatically noting the model and license number. One taillight was dimmer than the other. A sense of expectancy tugged at his mind.

The tan Chevy double-parked just past the cafe and the two men in the rear got out. One, stocky, with a heavy square face, was smoking a cigar. His companion was short, wiry, blond. They both appeared casual, unhurried, as they turned toward the cafe. Closing in on either side of Flash, they hustled him toward the waiting car.

Cassady cursed and reached for the door, pausing as a figure darted toward the Chevy from the opposite curb. *Turtleneck!* The wiry blond scrambled into the rear seat; his companion, cigar in mouth, shoved Flash in after him and followed. Turtleneck spoke hurriedly to the driver, darted away. The tan Chevy shot ahead.

Cassady gunned the Ford in pursuit, knowing he'd been made. The sour thought struck him that Geraci must have everyone on the street working for him. A pedestrian stepped out between two cars, leaped back as the tan Chevy shot past him, shook a fist angrily. Cassady tapped his horn and sped past.

The tan Chevy cut suddenly into the lefthand lane; the airhorn of an oncoming truck blasted angrily. The Chevy shot past two cars, cut back to the right with just inches to spare as the truck roared past. Cassady shook his head admiringly. No slouch, that driver.

He cut around the line of cars; the tan Chevy had gained a full block, now was hurtling across an intersection. He tromped on the accelerator, his mind racing. Pinto's men? They'd lead him nowhere . . . not while they knew he was on their ass. They'd have to shake him; until they did, Flash was safe. Safe? The two guys in the rear were probably working him over, getting information. If they did, Bennie was dead, dead. . . .

The Chevy's brake lights flared as an oncoming pickup truck made a left turn in front of it; the Chevy veered to the left, shot around the pickup and shot ahead again. Cassady grinned tightly. He was in his own milieu now. The driver of the Chevy was good, but not good enough. Hot pursuit was his baby. The tan Chevy screeched around a corner at high speed with Cassady on its tail.

The reflection of headlights in his rearview mirror momentarily blinded him. He jerked his gaze to the side mirror. The car behind was coming fast. Jesus, what now? A tail by its speed. Pinto? Pretty Boy?

He shot across an intersection, flicking quick glances at the side mirror. As the car behind passed under the street lamps he made it: *A Delta 88, gray, two-door* . . . the one he'd spotted behind him earlier. Another of Geraci's eyes.

The brake lights ahead flared again; the Chevy swept back into the empty left-hand lane. Warned, Cassady touched his brakes and edged into the same lane, anticipating the maneuver to come. A flick of his eyes at the side mirror showed the driver of the Delta had done the same. The tan Chevy made a long, sweeping high-speed turn to the right that gave it maximum radius and shot down a dark side street, Cassady screaming in pursuit. The Delta 88 clung to his tail.

Christ, if the car ahead stopped and blocked him, he'd be sandwiched! The flashing thought that they might be trying to set him up came to mind. He had to elude the tail without losing the Chevy. How? He suddenly realized that the Chevy's twisting run was taking him in the direction of the industrial area.

Orkie! An old warehouse over on Alameda near 22nd Street . . . a trucking firm—Garmont's words came back. *Not Orkie's style.* Yeah, he's said that too, but it damned well looked like he could be wrong.

Cassady pulled the scene into his mind, projected it into the immediate future. If the driver of the tan Chevy thought he'd eluded him he'd drop back to normal speed to keep from attracting the attention of a chance prowl car. How long to 22nd and Alameda? Five or six minutes. He'd have to risk it . . . if they didn't mousetrap him first.

The tan Chevy shot past a car nosing out from the curb, missing it by inches. The car jerked to a halt, its horn blasting—blasted again when Cassady shot past it, blasted a third time at the Delta 88. Approaching the next intersection the Chevy edged to the extreme right, its brake lights flared momentarily, then it went into a high-speed left turn and shot down another side street.

Cassady followed it through the maneuver. Jesus, that driver . . . as good as he'd ever seen. So was the guy tooling the Delta 88. Geraci must recruit his drivers from the Indy 500. He had to shake off the Delta . . . fast. The tan Chevy edged to the right again, its brake lights blinked and at the intersection it made another high-speed left turn. Now . . .

Cassady pumped the brake with four or five quick touches, saw the amber lights beneath the Delta's front grill wink in response. He edged to the left and almost at the intersection, began a turn to the right; the Delta tracked him. He suddenly jerked the wheel, began a sweeping turn to the left and midway hit the brakes. Tires screamed as the Ford's rear wheels went into a wild skid, bringing the nose around almost 180 degrees. Cassady swung the wheel hard, controlled the skid, felt the car shaking as the wheels grabbed for traction, completed the kind of U-turn he hoped he'd never have to make again.

He twisted around. The driver of the Delta 88, caught short, had hit his brakes early. For a brief moment, with the two cars only a few yards apart under the street lamps, Cassady had glimpsed the burly figure behind the wheel—the hard face, shadowy and indistinct, the shock of dark hair—before the Delta shot ahead, completed the left turn, was lost to sight.

Startled, Cassady tromped on the gas pedal again. He knew that face! *Who? From where?* It had been little more than a blur in the shadowy interior—enough to prod his memory, not enough to fill in the details. A face he'd seen on East Fifth? Someone he'd questioned? No, somewhere else. The heavy jaw, the thatch of dark hair. Wait, something . . . Jesus, the cheek! The scar livid under the pale light. *Dom Perrotti!* Instantly he coupled the identification with the anonymous phone call that had warned him about Pinto.

He suppressed his surprise. Homicide tailing him? No, the Delta had been parked near the cafe when he'd arrived. A stakeout! Yet a lieutenant wouldn't be on a stakeout; that was lower echelon stuff. But he had been. Why? The hell raised by the press? Had he gotten a tip? If so, it had to have been a damned hot one. Waiting to pick up Flash? Reasonable, if he'd been tipped that Flash knew Bennie's hideout.

The possibility brought a sense of urgency. Perrotti was getting too damned close! Cassady gripped the wheel. Damned if he'd let homicide move in now, beat him to the punch. Geraci was his baby. He pushed the thought from his mind to concentrate on the tan Chevy.

Had the driver shaken off Perrotti? Probably. The few seconds Perrotti had lost at the intersection would have been enough. By now the other should be tooling along at normal speed, congratulating himself.

Cassady resurrected a mental map and studied it, certain the other driver's destination was the warehouse. He'd have to cut to the right to intersect Alameda . . . or already had. Cassady visualized a dotted line on the map which would converge with the other's course. With luck . . .

He wheeled around a corner to the harsh squeal of brakes, the din of a horn; he sped flat out past a panel truck and through another intersection. No red light, no siren, and if some other bastard as crazy as he was came out of a side street . . .

A dozen blocks beyond he swung onto Alameda. Poor lighting, no pedestrians, traffic sparse—he floored the gas pedal again. If the driver of the tan Chevy had dropped speed—and Cassady was certain he had—he could scarcely have reached the warehouse yet. But it would be close. A sign under the blue-white cone of an arc light read *16th Street*.

A truck nosed out from alongside a loading dock and began a left turn. Cassady wrenched the wheel, glimpsed a frightened face gaping at him from the tractor before he cleared the front of the truck with but inches to spare. Harsh blasts from an air horn followed him. Sweeping past an old van he saw the taillights ahead . . . one bright, one dim. He let out a long breath; the Chevy appeared moving at normal speed.

Cassady kept the gas pedal floored. Suddenly the tan Chevy leaped ahead. He grinned mirthlessly, picturing the other's startled awareness. Before the Chevy could gain maximum speed, Cassady shot alongside it and swung the wheel to the right, glimpsing the alarmed look of the figure behind the wheel.

The driver responded instinctively, twisted the wheel and braked to avoid being sideswiped. Cassady swung the Ford away again, hit the brakes, watched the rearview mirror. The Chevy sideswiped the curb, went out of control, careened across the street. Brake lights flared. The driver wrenched the wheel, sent the Chevy into a wild rear end skid, tried to regain control and bounced off a power pole. The harsh sound of crumpling metal reached Cassady's ears as the Chevy came to rest halfway through a high board fence.

He made a sharp U-turn, sped back and skidded to a halt a dozen yards away. A sagging sign above the fence read *Maynard's Junkyard*. Scrambling out of the Ford, .38 in hand, he saw a blocky figure squeeze through the wrecked fence to the dark yard beyond. No sign of the driver or the short wiry blond. Nor of Flash. Crouching, he darted toward the Chevy, using it as a shield.

A furious deep-throated barking came from the front of the yard, came again . . . nearer. Cassady fancied he heard the swift padding of feet. More than one dog. He had a vivid mental picture of the big brutes racing through the darkness.

"*Heyer . . . for Christ's sake!*" The shrill, panicky scream was followed by the snarl of beasts. Two shots rang out in quick succession; the answering silence told Cassady the dogs were dead or dying.

Floodlights came on. Through the smashed fence he saw a jumble of cars—stripped, wrecked, crushed—but no movement. He slipped around to the side of the Chevy, gun ready, threw a glance through the open door. Groaning faintly, Flash was trying to push himself up from the floor. A siren howled in the distance.

Cassady hesitated momentarily. If Flash were pulled in, questioned, the dominoes would start falling; Perrotti would have Bennie within hours. No way! Geraci was his! The determination propelled him to action. He seized the Chicano by the collar, dragged him from the car. A five-second shakedown yielded a switchblade, then he slung the Chicano over his shoulder and raced toward the Ford.

"Please . . ." Flash uttered a thin wail of despair and struggled to free himself. Cassady shoved him into the front seat, raced around to the other side and started the engine. A quick glance in the rearview mirror showed red and amber lights flashing angrily in the distance. He swung around a corner and floored the gas pedal, conscious that Flash was pulling himself into an upright position. The sound of the siren died away and he reduced speed. The thought that Garmont wouldn't approve of his action brought a grim smile.

Cassady parked in the shadow of a tree. Switching off the engine, he probed the darkness around him before turning to Flash. The Chicano was staring sullenly ahead. Cassady sensed his rebelliousness. "Who were they?" he demanded.

"I don't know." The Chicano's voice was shaky, tinged with fear. "They just picked me up, hustled me into the car. Look at what one of those bastards did to my fingers . . . broke them." He raised a hand, wincing as he touched them.

"What did he want to know?"

"I don't know. Jesus, when the chase started they quieted down . . . just sat there like they were waiting to get killed. That guy at the wheel was a fucking maniac."

"While he was working on your fingers he was asking questions. What?"

"They thought I was someone else, honestly. They grabbed me by mistake."

"Who did they think you were?"

"Christ, I don't know. They just made a mistake."

Cassady constrained his anger. "Now I'll tell you what you do know: you know those birds were from the Syndicate and grabbing you wasn't a mistake and you also know what they wanted."

"Listen, if I knew I'd tell you, that's the truth."

"I'm running out of patience," Cassady warned.

"Why would I lie to you?"

"Okay, you asked for it." Cassady reached for the ignition key.

"What are you going to do?" Alarm flooded the Chicano's voice.

"Toss you back to those bastards. You're no good to me."

"Jesus, man . . .!"

"They'll still be trying to dig that Chevy out of the wood. I'm going to honk when I drive past, shove you out. If they made a mistake, like you say, they'll let you go."

"Christ, man, those guys would kill me!"

"So?"

"Someone told 'em I was asking questions, that was all."

"What kind of questions?"

"That was before I met you. The whisper was going around that they wanted Bennie and I thought I might pick up a couple of bills. I told you that before. I was just asking around."

"Trying to locate Geraci, right?"

"Jesus, man . . ."

"Do I feed you to them or don't I?"

"Give me a chance, man." Flash rustled gingerly in his pocket for a cigarette, extracted one and lit it. In the flare of the match his hands trembled; three fingers, badly swollen, undoubtedly were broken. He took a deep drag and exhaled. "Yeah, Geraci. I heard he was the top guy . . . the one who wanted Bennie."

Caught with a shrewd insight, Cassady eyed him. "You were trying to sell us both, weren't you . . . me and Bennie?"

"No, honestly!" The fright in the Chicano's voice told Cassady he'd struck it right.

"No?" He let the Chicano sweat for a few moments before continuing, "I know the answers to the next questions and if you don't feed them back to me right . . ." He let the threat hang.

"I won't lie, man."

"Who's Pinto?"

"He sees that guys pay off, I told you that."

"Just checking. Is he on my ass?"

"Yeah, like I said."

"Who's working with him?"

"Jesus, man, how would I know?"

"You hear things."

"Nothing like that, man. No one talks about that guy, and I mean no one."

"Is he Geraci's man?"

"I don't know, honestly. Jesus, who knows about that outfit? But he's up there, I heard that."

"Why didn't you sell us to him?"

"Not you, man!"

"Bennie then."

"I don't mess with that guy. No one does."

"Because he's a killer?"

"Christ, man . . ." Fright showed in the Latin's thin face again.

"Do you know the names of the guys who picked you up?"

"No way." Flash shook his head.

"Who do you think they were?"

"Maybe Orkie's men, I don't know."

"Why Orkie?"

"Well, he runs things too; that was just a guess."

"Where's Lois?"

"Lois?"

"Skousen's hooker."

"Oh, that Lois. I don't know, man, and that's the truth."

Cassady sensed an evasion, let it pass.

"Where's Bennie?"

"You promised me two C-notes," Flash whined.

"When I get Bennie. The address . . . let's have it."

"I don't know, man."

"Goddamnit, talk! You'd better know."

"It's down near 13th and Imperial, an old house. I never looked at the number."

"Okay, take me there."

"Not now, man. I've got to get to a doc; these fingers are killing me."

"Tough it out." Cassady felt no sympathy for him, certain he'd tried to sell him to Geraci. He glanced in the mirrors, saw the street behind was clear and started the engine.

Flash said nervously, "Where are you taking me?"

"To an old house, you remember; it's down near 13th and Imperial." As he pulled away from the curb Flash flung the door open and rolled out. Cassady grabbed for him, missed, hit the brakes. Before he could get out Flash had scrambled to his feet and was racing away in the darkness.

Cassady cursed, momentarily puzzled at why the Chicano had thrown away two C-notes, then it came to him: Finger-breaker had gotten his information. He cursed again. Flash had probably squawked everything he knew, now thought they might already be at Bennie's.

He weighed the possibility. Maybe, if they'd escaped from

the junkyard. Or they might be sitting in a small room, trying to explain the situation to a couple of dubious cops. Either way, Geraci was one up on him. Still, Flash hadn't known the street address; Bennie would be safe tonight. Or had Flash lied? A chance he'd have to take.

Near 13th and Imperial—that much jibed with what he'd gotten from the hooker. He started the car. But near could mean north, east, south, west. A small cafe, she'd said.

He spotted two near the dimly lit intersection, both counter affairs, empty. Cruising through the surrounding streets, he felt disheartened. There were scores and scores of old wooden houses, ranging from shacks to old-fashioned two-story affairs. Useless to try tonight, he knew. A stranger walking up to a dwelling on these dark streets could wind up dead.

Maybe tomorrow . . .

A soft rapping at the door brought Bennie Worth up from bed with a start. Frightened, he called, "Who is it?"

"Daisy . . ."

"Just a minute." Exhaling noisily, he felt the hammering of his heart, the cold sweat of fear. He slipped on an old gray bathrobe and shuffled to the door. Opening it a crack, he peered out. "What is it?" She was watching him expectantly.

"Aren't you going to ask me in?"

"Well . . ." He reluctantly opened the door. As she came inside, she darted her eyes around as if in search of something. A filmy housecoat scarcely concealed her thin, young body. She wrinkled her nose, sniffing. "God, it stinks in here. Don't you ever open the windows?"

"I was sleeping." He wondered if she thought he was a goat. Christ, he'd had enough of her yesterday to last a month. "Whatcha got in mind?"

She brushed back a lock of dark hair. "I heard something."

"Heard what?" Frightened, he felt the jolt of his heart, the fast thudding again.

"Some guys are after you, aren't they? That's why you're hiding out here."

"That's a lie!"

"Not according to what I heard."

"What did you hear?"

"It has something to do with a cop, something you know about."

"Who . . . who said that?"

"Marge. You know Marge . . . over in the Crystal Rooms. She got it from a guy named Ollie Madden. He has something to do with the Syndicate."

"Christ!" The sour taste of bile flooded his mouth. "What did he tell her? What did she say?"

"Not much." She sat on the bed and leaned back, propping herself with her arms. "At first he just asked if she knew you, had seen you lately, stuff like that, but you know Marge. She figured a guy like Ollie wouldn't be asking unless it was important, then she got him spilling in bed. That's when he told her he had to find you before the cop got to you."

"It wasn't anything, honest."

"That doesn't bother me, Bennie, but if Mrs. Hammond hears about it she'll toss you out. She's not about to get messed up with those guys."

"You won't tell her, will you?" He tried to hide his fright.

"You know me better than that, Bennie. I'm your friend." She tilted her head coyly. "Gosh, I hardly even charge you anymore."

"I know." He smiled gratefully at her.

"Maybe I can help you."

"How?"

"Well, if I knew what it was all about . . ."

149

"It wasn't anything, honest—just a misunderstanding."

"What about the cop?"

"I . . ." He floundered for words. "I knew a guy who got knocked off. I guess he thinks I know something."

"Do you, Bennie?"

"No, I told you that."

"That's not what Ollie told Marge. You know how guys like to talk in bed."

"Please, what did he say?"

"He said it had to do with Frankie Skousen, that guy that got all cut up." Her voice perked up. "It's about that reward, isn't it? Is the cop the one whose wife was killed?"

"Yeah, but I don't know nothin', honest. They just think I do."

"The Syndicate?"

He nodded miserably.

"They'll cut your throat, Bennie."

"Jesus!"

"You can't stay here." Her voice grew suddenly firm. "If those bastards come after you they'll murder us all. It ain't right, Bennie, putting us on the spot."

"Look, they can't," he protested. "No one's coming after me; I fixed that."

"Fixed it how?"

"I . . . I wrote a letter."

"What kind of a letter?"

"Well, it tells who did it . . . killed the babe."

"Who did you send it to?"

"I didn't yet, I still got it." His face brightened. "But I called someone, let 'em know."

"Smart man, Bennie." She got up and patted his cheek. "I was worried about you."

"You won't tell Mrs. Hammond, will you?"

"Not now . . . now that I know you got a letter." She patted his cheek again and turned toward the door. Watching her leave, Bennie felt his heart thumping like mad. Maybe when it was all over he should check with the doc.

Mae Hammond was waiting at the bottom of the winding staircase when Daisy came down. A wraparound robe covered her tall, angular body which, at forty-three, was surprisingly hard and muscular—a match for the taut, aquiline lines of her face. "What did he say?" she whispered fiercely.

"He . . . he knows something."

"Come to my room!" She grasped Daisy's hand and pulled her to a bedroom at the rear, then locked the door behind them. "What does he know?"

"Like you thought, he knows about that reward the cop is offering."

"What about it, girl? Speak up!"

"He knows who killed her . . . the cop's wife."

"Oh!" Mae Hammond released her grasp on Daisy's wrist and stepped back. "Who did he say did it?"

"He didn't, but . . ."

"You have to get that," she snapped. "What have you got a body for?" She swung a backhanded blow that struck the girl hard across the mouth.

Daisy recoiled, throwing up her hands. "Please, Mae, not my face!"

"What else did he say?"

"He said he was safe, they couldn't touch him."

"Why not?"

"He has a letter. . . ."

"What kind of a letter?"

"It tells who did it . . . killed the cop's wife. If they bother him the cops will get it."

"How do they know about the letter, did he say?"

"He called someone."

Mae Hammond stepped back musingly. "Then someone in the Syndicate did it."

"Maybe, I don't know. That's all he said."

"Enough, I think." She deliberated a few moments. "Later I'll tell you what we'll do."

"Please, I don't want to get mixed up with that bunch."

"You won't, it'll be safe. You've done fine, Daisy. You deserve a reward." She reached out and yanked the robe from the girl's thin body before she let her own wraparound drop to the floor.

Naked, she went to a drawer and brought out a whip.

Geraci puffed nervously at his cigar, stubbed it out in the tray beside him. Where was Kopke? He glanced at his watch: ten-fifteen . . . almost forty minutes since Kopke's call. What was detaining him, trouble?

He gulped the contents of his glass, rose and filled it again at the portable bar. *Orkie's men had snatched the Chicano*—that was all he'd let Kopke say before he'd cut him off, given him his address, ordered him over immediately. He'd have to teach Kopke about phones. The FBI had half the lines in town wired, regardless of what the government said.

What did the Chicano know? How much? However much, he must have gotten it from Bennie or the hooker. That damned Pinto should have had them both by now . . . and the cop. *Now Orkie knew!* He squeezed his glass savagely. Orkie would have the Chicano singing like a fucking canary. Jesus, the complications. He couldn't pull back now. He needed a clean sweep: Bennie, the hooker, the cop . . . Pinto. Yeah, and the Chicano. And if Orkie knew . . .?

He took another cigar from the humidor, lit it. Nothing Mark Kopke couldn't handle. He felt a faint reassurance. Kopke had jumped at the chance to grab Pinto's job . . . had swallowed the story about the Old Man having named him to clean up the mess. That was enough to button his lips for certain. And Kopke sized up as a real killer, as cold-blooded a son of a bitch as Pinto. Now he had to get Kopke moving.

A chime sounded softly. Geraci hurried to the intercom. "Yes?"

"Kopke."

Geraci pressed a button to unlock the front door, and waited. When the soft rapping came, he peered through the spy hole before admitting him.

"Sorry to be so long," Kopke said. "I twisted around a bit to make certain no one was on my tail."

Geraci looked sharply at him. "Did you think there might be?"

"Just a precaution."

"Smart. Care for a drink?" He gestured toward a chair.

"Yeah, a whisky . . . straight." Kopke stared in awe at the lavishly furnished suite before he moved across the deep plush carpeting in a manner that reminded Geraci of a cat slithering through tall grass.

Geraci stifled his nervousness while he poured the drinks. He couldn't allow Kopke to detect any sign of that. He had to be Angelo Geraci, the Old Man's strong right hand, and no questions asked. He returned, handed a glass to Kopke and sat opposite him. "What's the story?"

As Kopke related the incidents leading up to the crash, Geraci's mind was in turmoil. He started to speak at mention of Maynard's Junkyard, instead lapsed into silence. "The fuckin' dogs ripped Wheels' throat open before Heyer got a chance to shoot them," Kopke said.

"Wheels?" The name was new to him.

"A getaway driver. He's been with Orkie about a year."

"How about the Chicano . . . that Flash. Has Orkie got him?"

Kopke shook his head. "While Heyer and Madden were

busy with the dogs the cop snatched him, made off with him."

"Christ!" Geraci clenched his fists.

"No sweat. One of Orkie's people spotted the Chicano not long afterward. He must have jumped out of the car."

Geraci exhaled slowly. "Then what happened?"

"Heyer and Madden just made it out of there ahead of a couple of cops in a squad car."

"How about Wheels' body? They'll damned soon know."

"Naw, Heyer ditched it in a junked car at the other side of the lot. The cops will think the blood came from the dogs. Madden will cover the rest of it; no trouble there."

"And their car?"

"Hot. Wheels picked it up just a short time before."

Geraci hesitated. "How did Orkie know about the Chicano?"

"He was askin' questions about you; Orkie wanted to know why."

"Did he talk at all?"

"The Chicano? Yeah, after Heyer got rough. He told them where Bennie and the hooker were hiding . . . said he'd heard you wanted the information and he was trying to reach you."

"You got the address?"

"Both of them; they're not together. Heyer had to break a few fingers before he remembered that part."

Geraci suppressed a moment of elation. "What's Orkie doing about them?"

"I'm supposed to drag them in; that's why I called you first."

"You did right, Mark."

Kopke hesitated. "There's another angle."

"What?"

"Orkie got a call. The guy said he was Bennie—something about a letter."

"Letter?" Geraci felt a chill.

"The way I get it, the guy knows something. He told Orkie that if anything happened to him the letter would go to the cops."

"Christ!" Geraci fought his panic. That Jew bastard would pull something like that. But what would the letter be worth if he was dead? A dead man's word, and hearsay at that. But Jesus, the publicity alone could kill him. He brought his eyes back to Kopke. "What did Orkie say about it? Did he mention any names?"

"You mean about the call? He didn't talk much about it. I just happened to be there when he got it."

"I called him, too." Geraci watched him, mentally revamping his story.

"Orkie? He didn't mention that."

"Good, then we know he's closemouthed." Geraci lit a cigar to give him time to pull his story into line. How much would Kopke swallow? Enough, if the price was right. Set the price high enough and the details wouldn't matter; that much he knew. He replaced the lighter and said, "Orkie shouldn't have butted into this; you'll have to stall him."

Kopke watched him.

"I'm handling this on a strictly private basis for the Old Man, like I said. Some of our own people are involved . . . Pinto." He let the name hang.

"Yeah, he sure fucked up that Skousen job."

"The pointing finger." Geraci nodded. "And that's giving the Old Man big trouble. He's gone over a lot of names to find someone he knows can do what has to be done . . . and keep his lip buttoned. I told you that."

Kopke waited.

Geraci leaned forward and dropped his voice in a conspiratorial manner. "To handle this one you're going to have to know what it's all about, then you'll know more than anyone except me and the Old Man." He let his voice and manner convey a veiled threat.

"You don't have to worry about me," Kopke said.

"I know that, and so does the Old Man. He's checked you out. Handle this one right and you step into Pinto's shoes, and that's just a start."

Kopke's eyes remained expressionless. Geraci said,"There's a leak in the system—a big one—and the Old Man pinpointed it from a source high in the department. An assistant chief."

"Pinto?" Kopke's dark eyes flickered.

Geraci nodded. "They've got him on the hook on that Skousen job, now they're trying to use him to smash the Syndicate. The Old Man's the target."

"A deal . . . on that kind of a killing?"

"Think big, Kopke. Who was Skousen? A skid row junkie. A week from now no one will know his name. But Pinto knows enough to wreck the Syndicate . . . solve a dozen hits. You figure that one."

"Why not chop the bastard right now?"

"Because we need him to chop the cop, and Bennie . . . get that letter, if there is one."

Kopke tilted his head. "If the cops have him on the hook, would he chop one?"

"That's exactly what he'd do. You know why? The cop and Bennie are the two strongest witnesses against him. Neat, eh? Chop them and the cops will be left holding the bag. Pinto's a prick, Mark, but he's smart; don't underestimate him. Right now he's playing both ends against the middle but he doesn't know we're wise to him."

"I never did trust that runt son of a bitch."

"They both have to go, you can see that. So do Bennie and the hooker. Now here's the story. . . ." Geraci leaned forward and dropped his voice. "Skousen and a man presently high in the Syndicate killed the cop's wife. Does that surprise you?"

"Nothing surprises me," Kopke said.

"Nor me, Mark. But that's history, or was until the reward was offered. Somehow Bennie wheedled the story from

Skousen, probably for a fix—got everything but the proof. What probably happened is that he offered Skousen's hooker a cut if she'd get the proof, then act as a go-between with the cop. But she knew Bennie was a rat, would screw her out of her take. She's also a masochist, and Pinto was giving her what she wanted. In short, she cut him in on the deal."

Geraci watched Kopke's eyes as he spoke. Small, deep-set, unmoving, they reminded him of the eyes of a cat watching a mousehole.

"Then Pinto tortured the truth out of Skousen and killed him. That's what got the cops on him—his trademark; now they've got him by the nuts," he finished.

"He won't be missed," Kopke said.

"The Old Man's words, Mark. We have to get that son of a bitch before he brings down the whole house. Think you can handle it?"

"No sweat."

"We can still use the bastard. Give me the hooker's address and I'll have him take care of her tonight."

"Want me to handle it?"

Geraci shook his head. "Pinto would wonder why we sidestepped him. You're here for bigger things, Mark."

"How about Bennie?"

"We'll set him and the cop up for tomorrow, let Pinto dust them, then you take over. I just want to be damned sure that when the cops get there, they won't find a letter." Geraci felt the nagging worry again. Would that Jew bastard have passed it to some shyster lawyer or stuck it in a bank vault? "Tear that place apart," he added.

"From what the Chicano said, it's an old frame house down around 13th and Imperial," Kopke said.

"So?"

"Why not torch it afterward?"

"Great!" Geraci nodded approvingly. "You're thinking, Mark. A few gallons of gasoline sloshed around in the right places would take us off the hook. The Old Man will like that one."

Kopke hid his pleasure. "How about Augie Miller and Leo Hein? I heard Pinto has them working the job."

"They'll probably be there." He held Kopke's gaze. "They know too much, Mark."

"I never liked those bastards anyway."

"The cop will be there, too," he reminded.

"If someone tips him to the address he'll smell a rat," Kopke objected.

"Not this cop." Geraci smiled. "He's just a goddamned ticket pusher; he'll think he worked it all out in his peanut brain."

Kopke looked puzzled. "So how will we get him there?"

Geraci told him.

After Kopke left, Geraci sat in a stillness broken only by the low whisper of an air conditioner. Could Kopke pull it off? Cassady, Pinto, Bennie . . . and Miller and Hein almost certainly would be there. Still, if Pinto took care of the cop and Bennie, Kopke should be able to handle the cleanup. But how could he be certain there wasn't a letter in someone else's hands or in a vault? *That cop! That goddamned cop!* He clenched his fists savagely.

Fleetingly he considered the passport in his desk. He had money, plenty of it stashed away. Could he run fast enough? Far enough? The Syndicate had tentacles that reached everywhere. A vision of the Old Man—those implacable eyes in the wizened body—brought a shudder. No, he'd have to ride it out.

See it out! The decision came reluctantly. He looked down at Bennie's address. Besides, he had to be there to take care of Kopke. Do that and he'd be free.

The Old Man! Kopke felt a sharp exultation. *The Old*

Man had picked him! He kept his face blank, his eyes expressionless as he returned to his car. Pull this one out of the fire and he'd have it made. *Big Joe Orkie!* A malicious pleasure stirred him. In the future Orkie wouldn't look so big; not from where he'd be standing.

He allowed himself a faint smile.

10

CASSADY WOKE, TENSE AND edgy, the sound of plumbing rattling in the walls. *The chase, the car crash, the Chicano's panicky flight into the night*—the memories flooded back. If Flash had lied about knowing the address, Bennie could be dead by now; if he hadn't, Geraci's men would be shaking down the entire area.

He rejected the thought until he felt better able to cope with it. Sitting on the edge of the bed, he looked around the dismal room: tattered curtains, obscenities scrawled on the filthy walls, a few odds and ends of furniture that wouldn't sell at a flea market. He might as well have checked in at a flophouse.

Over breakfast he searched the morning paper. A small item on an inside page caught his attention: *High-Speed Chase; Guard Dogs Shot*. He scanned the article quickly. The car had been stolen; its occupants had escaped. Police believed the accident was related to a wild three-car chase through midtown only a few minutes earlier. Bare bones, nothing more.

He pushed the paper aside. No mention of Dom Perrotti's

involvement. Why? Because of the stakeout? Possibly, but what had put Perrotti onto the Chicano? How much did he know? How close was he to Geraci? Too close. Cassady gulped the last of his coffee and rose. He had to get moving. He paused in the doorway and scanned the street carefully before he started toward his car. No tails . . . yet.

Today was the day . . . if Bennie were still alive. He felt certain he was. Even the murder of a punk took time to set up—a thing that would be done in darkness. A knife, a wire around the neck. It would happen in a dismal room some- where. But today was the day. He knew it, felt it in his bones. Everyone was too close to Bennie—Orkie's men, Dom Perrotti, himself. And Pinto! He pictured the thin face un- der the dark snapdown brim. He couldn't afford to forget Pinto. Or Geraci. Somehow Geraci had become peripheral to the things that were happening, yet was the center of the storm.

Cassady pictured him behind a massive desk—the dark jowly face, the fleshy lips of a gourmet; soft, pudgy hands—a man who smelled of talcum powder and lime, but deadly for all that. Pinto to Orkie to Geraci—he fixed the steps firmly in his mind. Geraci at the top, in his big office . . . sweating. Close to panic. And when he broke, he'd come out. That was the moment Cassady was waiting for. Pulling into a loading zone, he found a public phone, dialed, waited.

"Southwest Investment . . ." The same girl's voice.

"Stick Geraci on the line!"

"One moment . . ." No hesitancy, no questions. He ex- perienced a grim satisfaction; Geraci, much as he dreaded it, was compelled to answer.

"Yes . . .?" Geraci's voice held a thick, glottal sound, as if his throat were constricted. Cassady pictured him clench- ing the phone, his pudgy face panicky.

"The word's around that Orkie's men are out to hit Bennie tonight."

"Orkie's men?" The words came sharply, filled with surprise. "Who is this?"

"I'll be there, Geraci, then I'm coming for you." A moment of silence followed before the sound of a receiver banging into its cradle echoed in his ear. Cassady walked out into the early morning sunlight and got into his car.

Orkie's men? There had been no doubt about Geraci's surprise. Because he'd penetrated the chain of command? No, it had been something else. The "something else" bothered him. But Geraci was near panic; his voice had fairly screamed it. And Geraci knew where he'd be tonight. At least he hoped he'd be there.

He thought of Cindy, wishing he could see her. Maybe a quick run over when she got off work. But he knew he wouldn't. Couldn't. Not till this was behind him, when he could go to her with the whole future ahead of them. Maybe tomorrow . . . but even tomorrow seemed a thousand years away.

Sighing, he pointed the Ford towards 13th and Imperial. More hours playing Lew Archer. But didn't Archer always get his man?

He tried to draw comfort from the thought.

Big Joe Orkie waited.

The dark eyes in the frail, lined face opposite him seemed remote, contemplative of things far removed from the subject of conversation, but Orkie knew such was not the case. The Old Man seldom strayed from the point. Rather, like a hunter hawk, he would circle for the right opening, then pounce. Orkie remembered his mother telling him of men like that when he was a child: men who saw what others couldn't see. Men spawned of witches. Maybe she hadn't been so superstitious at that.

Finally the Old Man stirred. "Think again, Giuseppe.

Was there nothing at all about the voice that struck you? Accent? Intonation? Choice of words?"

"A deep voice, masculine, like I said. I had the impression that he was big, a middle-aged man."

"Be more specific."

"Forty . . . fifty. He spoke just the two sentences, then hung up."

"Repeat what you told me . . . about the phone call."

"The phone rang . . ."

"Your private number?"

"No, the listed one."

"Repeat his words as exactly as you remember them."

"I picked up the phone and he said, 'Angelo Geraci has ordered Pinto to kill Officer Sam Cassady,' then before I could say a word, he said, 'The Old Man would want to know. Tell him.' Then he hung up."

"That was three sentences, Giuseppe."

"Oh, yeah, I didn't count the last."

"That can't be allowed to happen."

"The cop? No."

"Pinto has become an embarrassment."

"I'll take care of that."

"You have a man, Giuseppe?"

Orkie nodded.

The Old Man waited.

"Mark Kopke," Orkie said, "he's one of our collectors."

"No." The soft-spoken word was enough. Orkie mentally wrote off Kopke's future. The thin face had become still, the dark eyes thoughtful. Orkie wondered what was in his mind, marveled that he'd taken time to gather information and pass judgment on such a lowly worker as a collector. Eyes and ears everywhere. His respect for the other had become awe. He was suddenly aware that the dark eyes were fastened on him again.

"We will wait," the Old Man decided. "Perhaps this thing will take care of itself." Orkie had the distinct impression that he'd just been tested, but in what way he didn't know. A frail hand lifted and Orkie rose. "Thank you, Giuseppe, you have done very well."

His silver-haired escort appeared at some unseen signal. Thanking the Old Man for his audience, Orkie followed the other from the room. A faint smile touched the Old Man's lips. Orkie didn't understand, but he soon would; events would make them clear, he was sure.

He leaned back in his rickety chair to analyze this new information. A caller who knew enough about the Syndicate to know of him, and how to reach him . . . and of matters he knew would be of concern to him. And not the cop Cassady but Officer Sam Cassady. The faint smile came again. Dom Perrotti, certainly.

He resurrected an image of the young cop who'd faced him in the drab office, now more than twenty-two years ago. The steady voice, the lack of fear . . . in his eyes a sadness for his family; and the words: *I won't do a thing that will harm the force.* Hearing them then, he knew them to be true—a creed which but few men lived by. *The only guide to a man is his conscience*—words from some long-forgotten source. Now, by his act, Perrotti had declared himself Cassady's guardian angel. Yes, the two thousand had been wisely invested.

Cassady? If his information was right, and he was confident it was, Sam Cassady was another Dom Perrotti. In that respect it was quite unlikely that the Syndicate would be called upon to clean its own house. More than he could have hoped for. But there were intriguing aspects, too. Dom Perrotti, like Cassady, seemed to be pursuing a solitary course, neither offering nor seeking help from the other. Except for Dom Perrotti's call to Orkie, he amended; there was that exception. Perrotti, then, was convinced of Geraci's guilt and of his intent and, indirectly, had tossed the ball to him. But waiting, he decided again, was still the wisest course.

Was Cassady aware of Perrotti's support? Did he know and view it as a challenge? Did he know the name and position of the man he sought so relentlessly? Undoubtedly he did, yet still needed the one missing element: proof. Yet, almost certainly, he knew that the final proof would never be found with Bennie.

The Old Man leaned back, enjoying his mental soliloquy. It was, he reflected, like watching artists at work—artists who worked with the brushes of death. Cassady certainly had his eyes far beyond Bennie, yet Bennie was part of the pattern. But how did Cassady hope to draw his target into the web?

He contemplated the affair again, as he'd seen it when he'd made his decision. Cassady had spurned official help; that he knew from a source in the department. Neither had he passed on to his superiors any of what he'd learned. A loner, and such men were the most dangerous.

The Old Man nodded, satisfied. Cassady had no intention of delivering the man he sought into the hands of justice; there could be but one ending. He closed his eyes, sensing a momentary pain. Ah, Angelo . . . seldom had he been so wrong. That Geraci would even consider killing a police officer was unbelievable. Hadn't he considered the price to be paid? Had he taken on the mantle of a don without knowing how to wear it? Unforgivable. Now Angelo was alone. All alone.

He heard his *Consigliori* return, and said, "There's a dark raven in the sky, Arrigo."

"A great flapping of wings, but going nowhere, I'm sure," the other murmured.

"The wind is wrong," the Old Man agreed. He gave brief instructions before they left the drab office.

"Daisy? No." The hooker shook her head. Cassady thanked her and moved on.

"*Daisy? Never heard the name.*" The black girl behind the counter stared suspiciously at him.

"*Daisy?*" The old harridan in the manager's office eyed him shrewdly. "*Not here, honey, but I've got two lovely girls upstairs—Ivy and Marie.*"

From time to time Cassady paused to scan the street behind. No sign of the gray Galaxie or green Dodge. No sign of Pretty Boy or his companion, Ape; no sign of any tail whatever, yet not once had the sense of being under surveillance left him.

He paused at a corner to scan the block ahead. Ramshackle apartment buildings, ancient rooming houses, tumble-down shacks and shanties set behind makeshift fences—a duplicate of the blocks behind him, and those on either side . . . and somewhere Bennie. Enough to make even Archer despair.

The sun was westering when he bought an afternoon newspaper and settled for a shabby counter cafe on Imperial. A weary-looking waitress with hennaed hair took his order. Flipping through the pages to see if there had been any further developments on the junkyard crash, his eyes swept over an item, leaped back. *Slain Woman Was Skousen Friend.*

He scanned the story quickly: "*The body of a woman found knifed to death in a shabby East Ninth Street rooming house was identified by police as that of Lois Wilson, 28. Police named her as the woman who'd discovered the mutilated body of Frank Skousen, with whom she reportedly had lived. A spokesman for the Police Department said the possibility of a connection between the two crimes was being investigated.*"

His eyes skipped down the column. A cut throat . . . no suspects . . . a long record of arrests for drug and prostitution offenses. . . .

He pictured Lois Wilson's narrow face with its pale, blemished skin, eyes sunken deep in purple hollows. Why in hell hadn't she stayed at Cady's? Because he'd been too damned dumb to think about the monkey. He felt a twinge of guilt. Was he her keeper? No, but he should have known better.

He let the paper drop. Now that link was gone. That left only Bennie . . . if Bennie were still alive. He cursed softly. Geraci was digging the ground right out from under him. Pinto! And Garmont damned well knew that. So did Dom Perrotti. They knew plenty that they were holding close to their vests. Understandable, but it bothered him how much they might know, how close to Geraci they might be. If Perrotti worked his way through the tangle and nailed Geraci, it would be no more than an inconvenience to the bastard. Even if he were brought to trial—a farcical thought—he'd beat the rap.

No trial, he promised himself. It struck him again that he'd appointed himself judge and jury and hangman. *Cassady the vigilante.* Jesus, when he'd started in the Traffic Division he'd even winced at having to give tickets to doddering grandmothers whose mere presence behind the wheel was a threat to everyone on the road. Now he was contemplating murder. No, not murder. Not if Geraci faced him with a gun. If he panicked him enough, forced him into the open, the gun would be there in his hand. That was all he asked.

"Get you something else?" The hennaed waitress hovered over him.

"Yeah, Geraci."

"What?"

"Skip it." He slapped some coins on the counter and rose, uncomfortable with his thoughts. As he reached the door a figure across the street darted into an old apartment building. The abruptness of the move alerted him. His momentary impression had been of a short man, slender, dark curly hair, young. *Pretty Boy*! He hadn't had time to clearly discern the features but his subconscious mind had painted in the thick pouting lips, the receding chin.

Cassady wasn't surprised, but where was Ape? His hulking companion would be somewhere close by. What other eyes were on him? He looked along the street in both directions. No gray Galaxie that he could see. No green Dodge. At least Pretty Boy wasn't that careless.

He renewed his search, apparently oblivious of anyone in his wake, but with his senses attuned for the sound of footsteps, sudden movement. It struck him that the present area was the most unfriendly yet. An old hag spat at him and had slammed the door in his face; others had refused to answer his knock, although he'd heard movement inside. The faces and voices of those he accosted on the street were hostile, clouded with suspicion. He was the outsider. The stranger.

A prowl car swung around the corner ahead and cruised toward him. He was about to turn his back to the vehicle to avoid possible recognition when he caught the quick shake of the driver's head. Ed Durke, a graying veteran. The windows on the passenger side were rolled down.

Cassady halted by the curb and glanced casually around. Several bystanders were eyeing the car's approach. He turned his face from the oncoming car, apparently disinterested.

Durke stopped alongside him, picked up a clipboard and spoke into the radiophone as if making a report. "Some babe trying to reach you . . . Called the station three times today . . . the calls were transferred to Garmont, as per orders." Durke spoke slowly, clearly, spacing his sentences. "Garmont finally got her talking . . . Her name's Daisy . . . She said that Bennie has a letter that names the killer . . . She knows where he is and wants five thousand for the information . . . Garmont promised he'd have you there before night . . . She said she'd call back. Oh, yeah, all three calls were from different pay phones in this same general area. Watch your ass, Sam, you're hot."

Durke replaced the radiophone and clipboard, looked the other way and lit a cigarette. *Daisy would call tonight.*

Watching the prowl car pull away, Cassady felt a quiet desperation. By tonight Bennie could be dead. But a letter . . . As the implications struck him he felt a quiet excitement. Bennie had written himself an insurance policy! Had he gotten word of that to Geraci? He must have; he wouldn't have written the letter if he hadn't intended telling him. If so, Geraci would be in a real bind, have to call off his dogs. But the letter was . . . where? The question sobered him.

He tried to recall Durke's exact words. *Bennie has a letter. . . . She knows where he is and wants five thousand for the information.* Information about where he is, or where the letter is? Or both? Would Bennie be damned fool enough to keep it with him? Hiding out, would he have had a chance to put it in some safe place? Not likely.

Cassady drew a deep breath. Christ, it could be in his pocket or stuck away in some stupid place like under the mattress. If Geraci had received the same message, analyzed it in the same way, he couldn't get to Bennie fast enough.

He glanced around. The bystanders had drifted away. No tails that he could spot but the sensation of being watched persisted. Had anyone seen through Durke's act? Probably. He continued on his way while sorting his thoughts. At least Garmont had surfaced, undoubtedly had had him under surveillance from the beginning. To protect him, or to let him bird-dog the hunt? If he didn't show up at the station, would Garmont switch the call to someone pretending to be him to get the information? The son of a bitch would because he was all cop. He cursed savagely and glanced at his watch; he'd give himself till seven.

Later he caught sudden movement again, a glimpse in the periphery of his eye as he turned casually to look behind. This time his impression had been of a large man, big in the shoulders, stepping from view behind some shrubbery.

Ape? The incident brought the uneasy feeling of being hemmed in, maneuvered, set up. He turned along another side street, eyeing the old shacks and rooming houses ahead. Where in hell was Bennie?

The westering sun sloped down, a smoke-red ball of distorted shape in a smog-filled sky. Finally it vanished behind a row of old houses. For a while it left fiery fingers behind; then they, too, died away. Dusk sped in from the east.

Cassady felt his desperation return. Tonight *had* to be the night. If he didn't find Bennie tonight, Geraci's men would sever the last link. The letter? If Geraci knew about that, and Cassady felt certain he did, they'd tear the place apart, board by board. He glanced at his watch: he should be at the station shortly to wait for Daisy's call. Get it and a dozen prowl cars would be out there in five minutes flat, but that would still leave Geraci.

Why go? He all but paused in mid-stride. Geraci wouldn't be clear till Cassady was dead; Geraci damned well knew that. Whatever Geraci had planned for tonight, Cassady was part of it. He *was* being hemmed in . . . set up. By Pretty Boy and Ape and how many others? But Pinto would make the kill. Or try. If Cassady didn't get to them, they'd get to him. He smiled mirthlessly. Garmont could wait.

She came from a small house just ahead of him, crossed the weedy lawn and all but collided with him. Plump, blonde, around thirty-five, she was clutching a handbag that was slung from her shoulder by a strap.

"Hi," he said.

"Oh!" She paused as if seeing him for the first time. Caught in dusk, her face held a tight, wary look.

"Sorry if I frightened you."

"Just startled, that's all." She watched him guardedly.

"I'm looking for a girl named Daisy—short, thin, dark, about twenty-five."

"Daisy? Oh, *that* Daisy . . . if it's the same one."

"I'll check. Could you tell me where I might find her?"

"She lives on East 15th, down off Imperial . . . at 2110. That's 2110 East 15th." The words tumbled out fast—too fast and too rehearsed, Cassady thought. The fingers on the handbag were twisting nervously.

"You wouldn't happen to know if Bennie's with her, would you? Bennie Worth?"

"Oh, Bennie. I heard her mention the name, yeah." She glanced at her watch. "I have to go; I'm meeting someone."

"Sure, thanks." Amused, Cassady watched her withdraw. Not well done, and the quick way she'd pulled that address from the hat! He shook his head as she hurried around a corner. Eyes, voice, manner, everything about her had been phony. No doubt about it, he'd just been set up. But the address would be a good one; Geraci had seen to that. Two birds with one stone, the way he'd planned it. Now it was a question of which two birds.

He weighed her information against that he'd gotten from Durke. Had Daisy been trying to set him up? Had her spiel about a letter been a "come on" to make certain he'd bite? Had the plump blonde been thrown into the act when Daisy had failed to reach him? Entirely possible. Or was Daisy simply trying to collect? Equally possible, and in which case there could be a letter. In either event Pinto would be there . . . waiting, probably with Pretty Boy and Ape. It could prove quite a party.

Back at the parking garage he eyed his old Ford dubiously. By now everyone in the Syndicate probably knew it by sight. Well, he could change that. Twisting down the ramp, he headed toward a used car lot run by Chuck, a friend.

When he left the lot he was driving an old red Pontiac that should have been junked a decade before. "But she'll hold up for thirty days," Chuck had assured him, adding, "That's when the guarantee runs out."

"It's all set, Angie. That fuckin' cop won't see another day; neither will Bennie."

"I know, he called me."

"The cop?"

"He said he'd be there, the snotty bastard." Geraci clasped his hands to hide his nervousness from the thin, dark killer across from him, yet smug with the knowledge that it would be Pinto's last night, too. "He said word was going around that Orkie's men would do the job."

"Orkie's men?" Pinto looked puzzled. "When did he call?"

"This morning."

"Jesus, that was before the broad set him up."

"Then where did he get the address, tell me that?"

"Did he mention the address? Christ, he couldn't have, Angie. He's been pounding the pavement all day."

"Not the number, no, but he was damned sure he'd be there."

"Maybe something he got from the Chicano. The guy spilled to Heyer, so why not to the cop? Heyer flubbed that one, letting the cop grab him again."

"Maybe . . . " Geraci fretted inwardly.

"He put two and two together, that's all. The Chicano must have told him enough to make him certain he'd find the place by tonight."

"That doesn't explain how he knew Bennie would be hit tonight."

"Guessing, Angie. He figured that if the Chicano had spilled to Heyer, we'd be there. Maybe the Chicano recognized him as Orkie's man; that would explain that."

"Just so he's there."

Pinto sat back and made a steeple with his fingers. "Think he might show up with a load of cops?"

Geraci hesitated. "I doubt it, he wants to grab all the glory himself."

"That's the way I see it."

"We'd better be right, Pinto."

"If a bunch of squad cars pull up, we'll blow."

"Not till you get Bennie," Geraci said sharply.

"I don't intend to, Angie. That's a two-second job."

"Too damned many people are getting to know about this."

"No one who counts except the cop, and he won't be around to talk about it; that you can count on."

"How about the hooker—the one who set him up?"

"A nobody. She doesn't know who she was working for. All she knows is that she got a twenty for passing the information, and that someone was watching to see that she did. It's foolproof."

"That still leaves the Chicano."

"Does it? I heard he got it somewhere; probably some junkie with a knife."

"Nice work." Geraci smiled placatingly to hide his relief.

"I wouldn't know how it happened, or to the hooker, either. I was playing cards with a few of the boys at the time."

"Of course." Geraci brought up his eyes, wondering if he should mention the letter. It was the kind of dynamite he hated to place in Pinto's hands. The bastard was getting too overbearing as it was. But if there was a letter. . . . "Something else occurred to me," he said finally.

Pinto lit a cigarette and waited.

"Bennie might have been smart enough to put something in writing."

"If he did, he'll talk. No trouble there."

Geraci glanced at his watch. "That cop might have headed right for the place."

"Great, then he'll walk right into Augie and Hein." Pinto gestured nonchalantly and rose. "Stop sweating, Angie, your collar's all wet."

When the door closed behind him, Geraci got on the phone, waited briefly till Kopke answered, and said, "Everything's set."

"I'll let you know. . . ."

"I'll be home . . . waiting." Geraci replaced the phone and lit a cigar, feeling a curious relief. Kopke wasn't a sadist like that damned Pinto, but he sensed he was far more ruthless, and with the reward he'd dangled. . . . No, none of them would walk out of there alive, he was certain.

No one would walk out of there alive! Geraci was pleased with himself. He'd be there to make certain of that. He'd scouted the street earlier, located the house, planned the sequence of actions—as foolproof as anything he'd ever laid out. The final touch, and that was it. With Kopke dead, his own trials would be over.

He thought of his call to Orkie and worry momentarily clouded his mind. Had Orkie passed the message to the Old Man? He would have, that was certain, but if the Old Man had had any suspicions about him he would have been summoned by now. No, he'd laid the whole thing on Pinto's shoulders and the Old Man had bought it; on that score he was safe. After tonight he could start living again. The contemplation brought a feeling of exhilaration.

Dom Perrotti slipped out from his car and squinted down the dark, silent street as if sighting along a rifle barrel. Ahead, Pinto appeared to be gliding through the night, a slight, indistinct figure nearly a half-block away.

Perrotti followed, keeping to the deepest shadows, careful to avoid the occasional splashes of light from nearby windows. Mindful of the area through which he was passing, he kept his senses attuned to his sides and rear while watching the fleeting shadow ahead.

Abruptly Pinto stopped and Perrotti sensed his careful scrutiny of the night. Finally he moved again, became lost in the darkness of a large, overhanging tree. Perrotti heard the low murmur of a voice, looked slowly around, saw the glow of a cigarette on a nearby porch. Crossing the street, he proceeded stealthily to a position almost across from where he'd last seen Pinto. Beyond, near the end of a deep lot, the roofline of an old two-story house jutted against the sky. The backlighted blind in the narrow window of a high Victorian turret marked the structure as a relic from an age long gone. A second groundfloor light at one side near the rear was visible through the web of a large pepper tree.

Perrotti felt certain that Pinto had reached his destination. Bennie's hideout? If so, goodbye, Bennie, and the world would be better off. He felt a grim satisfaction: if Pinto pulled this one, he'd be right there to grab him. No card game with friends this time.

Movement under the dark tree caught him, then Pinto came briefly into view as he crossed a weedy patch before plunging into the darkness of the trees fronting the house. Perrotti marked the location before returning to his car, an old Plymouth he was using in the off-chance that his Delta might be recognized.

As he drove past the old house his headlights caught the scarcely decipherable numbers *2110* on a lopsided board tacked on a post near the curb. He circled the block, parked behind Pinto's Buick, rustled a wire from under the seat and got out. Working the wire through the front window, he hooked the release latch and opened the door. A quick check of the glove compartment and the car's interior revealed nothing compromising, but neither had he expected to find anything. Pinto, on the hunt, was a careful man.

Before returning to his car he scanned the block again. Old rooming houses, smaller structures set behind rickety fences, lawns no more than weed patches—an area that looked and smelled of crime and decay. No pedestrians visible, but in this neighborhood people seldom walked the street at night; not even those who lived here.

Perrotti drove slowly, this time studying the cars parked along the curbs—a scrutiny that was caused by an unrest in his subconscious. Near the end of the next block a green four-door Dodge brought instant familiarity—the car that Leo Hein and Augie Miller had gotten into at Gino's, after they'd split from Pinto.

His mind leaped back. He'd been tailing Pinto when he'd witnessed the meeting at the pizza house. Immediately afterward Pinto had driven directly to the Crossman Building, which housed Geraci's offices; it had been that combination which had alerted him, brought the feeling that the search for Bennie was nearly at an end. Now all three were here. He felt a tightening of his scalp.

At the next intersection he rounded the corner and circled back, this time parking close enough to the old house to afford him a fair view of the less dark weedy patch in front. He rolled down the windows to listen; the only sounds were those borne in from a distance.

Lights in the rearview mirror flashed in his eyes. He brought his head around sharply. An old red Pontiac rattled past. A single occupant. He watched the Pontiac cross the next intersection, become lost to sight. He lit a cigarette, shielding the glare of the match in the cup of his hands before he settled back to sort the pieces.

Pinto, Hein, Miller—he didn't like the combination one damned bit. Syndicate punks, but dangerous. Hein's reputation as a hit man, like that of Pinto's, unfortunately had never been proved. Augie Miller was smaller fry, but almost certainly gutsy. Of the three, Pinto was by far the most dangerous.

Perrotti reflected on what could have brought them together in this dismal neighborhood. Bennie, probably, but two hit men and an on-the-job learner for that cheap punk? Geraci must have hit the panic button. He shelved the reflection, knowing that wasn't it; the arithmetic was all wrong. That wasn't Pinto's style, never had been. A loner if there ever was one. So what had brought the three together?

He shuffled the pieces into a picture, tried to bring it into focus. Pinto's earlier meeting with Hein and Miller, his later meeting with Geraci—now Pinto, Hein and Miller here, waiting. *Waiting*! As the word clicked in his mind, the picture slid into focus.

Cassady! *A setup*! It had to be! Perrotti felt an inner coldness. *Tip Cassady to Bennie's hideout . . . and wait*! The old lure. Christ, how many guys had gotten burned on that one? *Sam, are you biting*? Yeah, he'd bite. Intrigue wasn't Cassady's field; he was a traffic man. And just now, too damned anxious to nail someone to the cross. He'd come running.

Perrotti considered the situation. Had Cassady heeded his anonymous warning about Pinto? More likely he'd taken it as just another crank call. Like a horse with blinders, he was looking in just one direction . . . straight ahead. He'd grab the tip, walk in like a big fat pigeon. All he wanted was Bennie, alive and singing, and not down at headquarters, either. Cassady had to be stopped before he tackled this one. He was going to be mighty unhappy about that.

Movement! He peered into the night, trying to detect whatever it was that had alerted him. He scanned the dark lot, the darker trees beyond, the old house. The stillness seemed complete. A trick of the eyes? His imagination? No, he glimpsed it again, the briefest of movement, scarcely more than a dark blur against a darker background.

Perrotti fixed the spot—deep shadows near where the light from the ground floor filtered through the pepper tree. A perfect spot from which to watch the front approach to the house. That would be Miller or Hein, with the other at the rear. He had to give Pinto high marks for being careful. He'd be inside now . . . cutting Bennie's throat.

He sized up the old house critically, attempting to visualize its interior geometry. Most old structures like this had long since been carved up into cheap rooming houses or, in this area, more likely cat houses. In either event there should be others inside. Yet only two lights—one low, the other high in the turret. The reflection troubled him.

Perrotti brought his gaze back to the street. *Where was Cassady?* Close. The knowledge came with that inborn sense he'd long ago learned to trust. Maybe Cassady wasn't such a big pigeon after all, was taking the time to look the place over before he moved in. Jesus, he had to spot him before he set foot on that goddamned lot. His nerves felt suddenly tense, edgy, expectant. Crushing out his cigarette, he slipped from the car and patted the .38 in his shoulder holster. Pinto hadn't planned well enough. He hadn't counted on Dom Perrotti.

11

CASSADY PARKED THE PONTIAC under a tree, several blocks from the address given him for Bennie. Getting out, he located several successive numbers. Calculating that Bennie's hideout would be on the right, the third block down, he returned to the car.

The starter made a harsh clattering sound before the engine caught, coughing awhile until it settled down into its noisy rhythm. He reflected that a one-day guarantee would have been stretching it, but at least it looked at home in the area.

He crossed the second intersection and reduced speed, conscious that eyes might possibly be watching his passage. One pass, that was all; he had to spot the place the first time through. An old wooden house, Flash had said. Only they were all old, all wooden. Archer would have pinned that one down. Disregarding the cars parked along the curb, he scanned the shadowy structures at his right.

There . . . 2110! He'd almost missed the number tacked lopsided on a post as the Pontiac rattled past. Swiveling his head around sharply, he glimpsed two lighted windows—one set high, the other at ground floor level on a side near the rear. His instant impression was of a rambling two-story house set well back among trees. He flicked his gaze back: six houses from the corner.

He crossed the intersection, his attention on the cars parked along the curbs. Near the end of the next block he spotted a green four-door Dodge and tabbed it instantly: *Pretty Boy's*. He wasn't surprised that Pinto had brought company. Undoubtedly Ape was there, too. Cassady grinned humorlessly. Circling the block, he noted that the houses were set back to back, with no alley between.

Parked on the adjacent street, six houses from the corner, he rolled down the window, studied the darkness, listened. Most of the dwellings showed subdued lights through the window shades; the only sound was faint music from a radio or TV. The house nearest—which he judged to be back to back with 2110—was disconcertingly well-lighted in front but the rear, as far as he could discern, was dark. The next house had a lighted window on the side nearest him.

He got out, crossed a weedy lawn and moved between the houses with a silent prayer: Please, no dog. Beyond a junk-littered yard the old two-story house jutted above its sentinel trees. He studied the yard carefully before crossing to a sagging board fence at the rear. Positioned in the black shadow of a tree, he let his eyes rove slowly over the yard opposite him. Past fifteen or twenty feet of weed-covered ground another border of trees all but hid the lower part of the house.

The feeling of *presence* was strong. No sound, no movement that he could discern, yet he knew that a watcher was there. Pretty Boy or Ape, he decided. One would be covering the front, the other the back. Pinto was probably already inside . . . with Bennie.

Too late, too late—he let the refrain drum in his mind before closing it out, returning his scrutiny to the house. From his present position the only light visible came from a lower shaded window, its pale beams filtering through a pepper tree. A top corner of the blind had been ripped and sagged inward.

He studied the profile of the house, trying to translate it into a map which would tell him something of the interior. Probably a couple of bedrooms downstairs, three or four more upstairs. A whorehouse, according to Flash. What if there was a madam, several girls, perhaps a few customers? How would Pinto handle that? The question struck him as whimsical. But the large bulk of the house, darkened, mitigated against that.

Cassady felt in no hurry; Pinto would wait. Did he know about the letter? Probably not. And Daisy . . . where was she? He returned his gaze to the yard, looking for some sign of Pretty Boy or his sidekick.

He stiffened at the sudden barking of a nearby dog. In that same instant he caught a small glow describing a short arc; it took him a moment to place it as the burning ember of a cigarette moving with the swiveling of a head. Abruptly the barking ceased, the silence returned—an unnatural silence to Cassady. Deep, all-pervasive, it seemingly smothered the dark world in which he stood. The glowing ember had disappeared. Tense with anticipation, he subconsciously held his breath for a long moment before he slowly exhaled.

Either Pretty Boy or his sidekick, he decided. But what had alerted the dog? What had so suddenly silenced it? He felt vaguely uneasy. Something was happening beyond his ken, but what? He groped for a stone, found one and threw it into the yard where he'd heard the dog. The stone struck with a dull thud; no other sound followed.

Time to get moving, he decided. He pulled himself over the fence, dropped into the darkness under the tree, crouched and slipped the .38 from its holster. Motionless, he watched and listened, his hand sweaty on the gun. He felt sweat, too, on his brow, his body, his nerves keyed to a high pitch. Finally satisfied that the yard was deserted, he darted across a weed-covered patch into the deep shadows beyond.

He jerked suddenly backward, his finger tight on the trigger as he discerned the dim outline of a body on the ground. Expecting gunfire, he twisted violently away, swung around in a crouch, brought up the .38, stayed the finger on the trigger at the sight of the pale blur of a face, an outflung arm limp against the dark earth.

He threw a quick look around before he drew a pencil flashlight from his pocket and knelt alongside the prone figure. Shielding the red beam, he studied the other's face: Pretty Boy wasn't so pretty anymore. Blue eyes vacant, pouting lips slack, neck a gory mess. He rolled the head to one side; the back of the skull had been brutally crushed. The cut throat had been added insurance that Pretty Boy wouldn't recover.

Cassady opened the coat. A short-barreled .38 snugged in a shoulder holster made it clear that Pretty Boy hadn't been expecting an assault. From an inside pocket he drew out a wallet and flipped through it. The name on the driver's license was August T. Miller. He automatically noted the birthdate: Pretty Boy had just made his thirtieth and final year.

He replaced the wallet, snapped off the beam and rose. Why Pretty Boy? That didn't make sense. He struggled to pull together the elusive thoughts that tumbled through his mind. Pinto to Orkie to Geraci—that was the hierarchy as he'd seen it; now Pretty Boy was dead. Who had killed him? Why?

Orkie's men? The thought came unbidden and he examined it, sensing something that as yet lay beyond his awareness. He recalled Geraci's surprise when he'd told him that Orkie's men would hit Bennie. Why the surprise? Was it possible that Orkie wasn't involved? Yet Flash's captors had certainly been headed toward the warehouse which, according to Garmont, served as Orkie's headquarters. Okay, Orkie was involved, but how? Would he have risked the snatch merely because he'd heard that Flash had been asking around about Geraci, as the Chicano had claimed? Maybe, but he sensed something more.

"That's not Orkie's style, Sam." Cassady swore softly as he recalled Garmont's words. He'd listened to Garmont without hearing him. Garmont had decisively ruled Orkie out in any part of Skousen's murder, had just as unhesitatingly pointed the finger at Pinto. Was Pinto working directly for Geraci? It seemed so.

What else had Garmont said? *"The Syndicate keeps a damned low profile, Sam; Orkie's job is to keep it that way."* Would Orkie go so far as to order murder to stop Pinto tonight? He looked down at the body—the crushed skull, the cut throat. Pretty Boy would damned soon be identified as having been a Syndicate hood, then—Bingo!—the spotlight would be right where Orkie didn't want it. Not Orkie's men then, but who?

Geraci to Pinto . . . period. But why the murder of Pretty Boy? The order, if his reasoning were right, must have come from Geraci. But if he'd had Pretty Boy killed, why not Ape? And if he were trying to cover his tracks, why not Pinto? That would indicate another killer on the scene—someone more trusted.

Cassady knew exactly what he should do—he should get a SWAT team here on the double. He sensed an immediate conflict. Bennie almost certainly was dead, but there was still the possibility of a letter. If Pinto had gotten it . . .

He knew what would happen, clearly. Get a SWAT team and goodbye letter—Pinto would destroy it immediately. But was there a letter? He had to assume there was, and *if* there was, he damned well wanted it. Neither would Pinto surrender; he'd come out with a blazing gun. By the time it was over the whole bunch would be dead and Geraci would walk away free and clear. No way was he about to let that happen. Sam Cassady—judge, jury and hangman. He didn't like the sound of it.

He studied the rear of the house again. A shadowy door led to what appeared to be a screen porch; beyond would be a kitchen. With Pinto waiting? The door was too tempting. He switched his attention to the lighted shade in the lower room. A bedroom? The torn blind was too high to peer through but if he climbed the pepper tree . . . He looked at the dim light filtering through one side. He could stay clear of that.

Okay, Pinto, I'm coming. He reached the tree on the dark side, tested the lower branches, then pocketed the .38 and pulled himself up. Balanced on a thick limb, he skirted the lighted area and climbed to a branch above the window. He eyed it dubiously, wondering if it would support his weight. Only one way to find out, he decided. Edging out on it, he felt it bending under him, then grasped the edge of the window frame to steady himself. Peering through the tear in the blind, he suppressed a startled gasp.

A nude young woman lay sprawled face down on a bed, her arms clasped around her head as if trying to protect herself. Her back and the blankets under her were a bloody mess. Another nude woman, far older, with the muscular build of a man, lay crumpled on the floor, a whip next to an outstretched hand. Both dead, he knew. Jesus, someone had loosed a homicidal maniac!

Pinto! The name crashed in his mind. Pinto hadn't wanted to be disturbed while working on Bennie. He wouldn't bother to tie them, gag them; murder came too easily. Now he'd be in the turret room. Neither did he expect to be disturbed.

Cassady examined his reasoning. The two bodies would alert any intruder; Pinto wouldn't have missed that point. It followed that he hadn't expected anyone to get that far; Pretty Boy and Ape were to see to that. Only Pretty Boy was dead. The back door . . .

Cassady started to climb down when he caught the sound of movement and froze. Pretty Boy's murderer? Ape? Peering down through the branches, he saw someone come to a halt a few feet off to one side. Tall, bulky in the shoulders. Ape going back to check with Pretty Boy? And when he found the body?

He stifled the impulse to reach for his .38. The slightest movement could cause the branches to tremble, the other to look up. If he did, scratch one traffic cop. Cassady felt the sweat break out anew.

He became aware that the other had turned back toward the front yard, his head cocked in a listening attitude. Christ, had he sensed him? Scarcely daring to breathe, Cassady kept his gaze riveted on the figure below, prepared to hurl himself downward should the other glance up.

The man's head was swinging slowly, like a radar scanning the night, then stopped again, cocked in a listening attitude as he moved slowly into a half-crouch. A hand came up, holding a gun; in the dim light Cassady saw the bulky silencer on the muzzle.

Geraci took the 7.62 Luger from the glove compartment and checked the magazine before screwing the big, perforated silencer on the barrel. Thrusting the weapon into his coat pocket, he moved out from behind the wheel.

For a few moments he waited, testing the darkness around him. Although he'd only been in this particular neighborhood once before, when he'd driven through it to case Bennie's hideout, it brought a flood of familiar memories that eased his tension. Odors, dilapidation, sense of threat—all were reminiscent of the streets of his youth.

For some reason he remembered—when he was eight? nine?—running home, crying, after some older boys had waylaid him while coming from school, calling him a goddamned "wop" and "dago" and beating him up. His father had been angry with him, disdainful. ("*Running away, Angelo? For shame! For shame!*") Then he'd brought out a knife, pressed a button and a gleaming blade snapped out. "*Here, next time use this.*"

The following afternoon the same boys waylaid him again. He vividly recalled the fright on their faces when he'd yanked out the knife, snapped open the blade, slashed the arm of the biggest boy before they'd raced away, terrified. On that day "Dandy" had been born.

The word had spread quickly: "*Don't fuck with that wop; he's mean.*" Thereafter they'd given him wide berth. Almost simultaneously he'd become the unquestioned leader of the neighborhood boys of his own age group. Soon they all had switchblades. *Strike first and fast!* Geraci had never forgotten the lesson; indeed, it had propelled him up and up and up.

He started toward the old house, some three blocks away. Walking along the dark street, he fancied he could picture the kind of people who lived in each shadowy structure around him, and what was happening behind the drawn shades. Did one ever shed his origins? He could imagine how they'd feel if they saw him, knew who he was, the power and status he commanded. Envious and admiring, for long ago he'd learned that was how ghetto dwellers regarded one of their kind who'd made the long climb upward.

He also knew enough to keep a hand on the Luger.

Closer to the old house, he became more cautious. Abruptly he caught movement in the shadows by the curb and halted, gripping the weapon. Someone getting out of a car. The figure remained still for a few moments, as if assessing the darkness around him. Geraci had the impression of a big man, bulky, but when he headed toward the old house his movements were like those of a cat. Finally, close to the lot where the old house stood, he vanished into the darkness under the trees.

Geraci approached the car, a dark, two-door Plymouth that had seen better days. Glancing around, he opened the door. The glove compartment held several pencil stubs, a beer can opener, a miscellany of trash that told him nothing. He was about to withdraw when he spotted a radiophone tucked on a shelf under the dashboard on the driver's side. An undercover car.

Cassady! His heart began to pound. Cassady . . . moving into the trap! Visions of the scenes-to-be leaped into his mind. Hein and Miller would be covering the front and back, waiting for the cop while Pinto took care of Bennie. As soon as their work was done, Kopke would do the rest. And if he couldn't find the letter . . .

Geraci envisioned the old wooden house exploding into a raging inferno. It would go up like straw, reduce everything in it to ashes; the police might never identify the bodies. Not those inside. In any event, the whole thing could be laid to Pinto.

He peered at the darkness under the trees where he'd last seen the other. Cassady was probably still there, sizing up the place. Not even a traffic cop would be stupid enough to barge right in. Stupid? Cassady, for some reason, gave him an uneasy feeling. But however he did it, the end would be the same.

Geraci gripped the gun. He couldn't afford to get careless. He scrutinized the house for several minutes, noting the open patch of weeds, the trees in front and along the sides, the ground floor light near the rear and the one showing through the high turret window. He had to move in close, be in position when Kopke came out. He visualized him running, outlined by the crackling flames which leaped skyward behind him. His sole thought would be to get away. Geraci snickered. It would never occur to Kopke that Geraci had other plans for him. With Kopke dead, his own nightmare would be over.

Had he missed anything. Geraci ran the sequence over in his mind, as carefully as a statistician plotting points on a curve. The letter! That damned letter! He'd almost forgotten that. There was always the chance that Kopke would find one, bring it out. He'd have to check his pockets—and keep an eye peeled for that damned cop.

Quietly, watchful, he skirted the position where he believed Cassady to be and approached the old two-story structure from the far side.

Perrotti spotted movement under the large trees at the front of the house. It struck him more as a slow shifting of shadows, dimensionless, rather than a thing of form or solidity. Instead of leaping into his awareness, it seemed to have crept there. Wind in the trees? He glanced up at the branches limned against the sky; in the warm, muggy air they were absolutely motionless.

He looked back at the darkness below. Several minutes passed before he detected movement again, this time lasting only a second or two, and in a slightly different position than before. Hein or Miller growing restless, impatient, he decided.

He glanced both ways along the dark street. Where was Cassady? He had a prickly, uneasy feeling, a clamoring in his senses but with no identification of cause. Some subliminal sound? Something detected by eye that had failed to register? Cassady—it had to be. If he were trying some cute approach, he could walk right into Miller or Hein, never know what hit him.

Perrotti studied the dwellings on either side, the dark patches around them, the weed-covered front yards. No one sitting on a porch that he could discern. He drew a mental map: a flank approach would offer the best cover. He returned his gaze to the spot where he'd last detected movement. If he'd brought in a SWAT team, as he should have, they'd have nailed the whole bunch by now. But by next morning, he was sure, the chief would receive an anonymous envelope containing the damning infra-red pictures. Silently he cursed his past. He had to move in, take out whoever was there before Cassady blundered in.

He crossed the front yard to the nearest house, edged along the porches until he reached the corner of the dwelling which bordered the lot where the old house stood. The side position afforded him a clearer view. Several large trees near the curb; behind, an open area overgrown with weeds, a few sparse bushes and, farther back, other large trees that shielded the front and sides of the structure. At best he still had twenty or so feet of open space to cross, only he'd be dead before he got halfway.

Perrotti was pondering his predicament when movement in the periphery of his eye brought his head sharply around. It took him a moment to place it as a figure passing through the pale beams that filtered through a pepper tree. Subconsciously he measured the figure against the height of the window, had the impression of a big man—far too big for Miller, he decided; it had to be Leo Hein. Going back to check with Miller?

Perrotti made an instant decision without pausing to weigh it. Drawing his .38, he sprinted in a zigzag crouch across the weed patch and halted under the trees, breathing heavily. What if Miller had been stationed at the front and Hein had been returning to his post at the rear? He cursed himself for a damned fool, but he'd lucked out.

He switched the weapon to his left hand and brought out a sap. Hein, when he returned, would have a welcoming party. Glancing around for a more secure place to hide, he spotted a figure on the ground. Startled, he plunged to one side, landed hard and twisted around, his finger tight on the trigger when he realized the figure hadn't moved.

Cassady? Had Hein gotten him? Fumbling in his pocket for a pen flashlight, he moved swiftly forward, crouched by the prone body. After a quick glance around, he shielded the beam and flicked it on just long enough to look down into the dead face of Leo Hein, the gore that covered the swarthy neck.

Perrotti rose slowly, gazing toward the pepper tree. The big figure he'd glimpsed had to be that of Cassady. Christ, Cassady had flipped; no way could he explain a cut throat.

His mind raced. He'd underestimated Cassady badly. Cassady had cased the place, had spotted Hein and Miller, now was slipping back to get Miller before he went for Pinto. Or was Miller already dead? Jesus, Cassady had to be stopped. Stop him now and maybe they could hash up something to explain the cut throat.

He started toward the rear of the house, had taken but a few steps when his eye caught movement under the pepper tree; simultaneously he felt a violent shock that drove him backward. A dim *phut-phut-phut* reached his ears as he reeled and fell.

"Cassady! For Christ's sake, Cassady!" The scream was torn from his lips as he struck the ground and blackness came.

Startled, Cassady lifted his head. Through the branches he saw a shadowy figure reel and fall. *Perrotti!* He knew it instantly. He scarcely breathed as the figure below whirled around, looking for a second assailant.

Cassady grimaced. Perrotti's cry had tipped the man below, now he was expectant, alert. How had Perrotti known? He cursed silently. Everyone must have been right on his tail from the beginning, both police and Syndicate. He fought the impulse to reach for his .38. Do it and the branches would tremble, the other would look up.

Abruptly the dark figure below withdrew silently toward the rear of the house. Cassady drew the .38 from his pocket. When certain it wasn't a ruse to draw him out, he untangled himself from the branches and dropped to the ground. Faced in the direction the other had taken, he peered into the darkness and listened. No sound. No movement. Crouched, he ran to the body sprawled in the shadows.

Perrotti was lying face up, arms outflung, one hand gripping a .38, a sap in the other. Glancing quickly around, Cassady brought out a pencil flashlight. The thin red beam disclosed a bloody groove in the scalp, a bloody froth at the lips. He loosened the jacket and ripped open the shirt; blood welled from a wound near the heart. He doused the beam and grasped Perrotti's wrist; the pulse was weak, irregular. If he could get help fast enough . . .

He rose quickly, looked at the nearest dwellings. All were dark, as if their occupants had sensed trouble. He knew he'd get no help from any of them. His best chance was the old house. Pinto would have heard or Ape—it had to be Ape—would have gone in through the back to warn him. Fuck 'em! He raced around to the front porch.

The old-fashioned door was heavy, solid, with a small oval of leaded glass at eye-level. He tried to twist the knob. Finding it unyielding, he placed the muzzle of the .38 against the lock and fired. Metal grated as he twisted the knob again and kicked the door open. Leaping inside, he half-expected Pinto and Ape to be waiting.

Nothing moved in the darkness. No sound from the rooms beyond, nor from upstairs. What had Pinto done when he'd heard the crash of gunfire? Had he thought it was Pretty Boy or Ape disposing of him? No, they'd been using silencers. *Pinto knew he was inside . . . and where in hell was Ape?*

Pretty Boy! Memory of the dead face flashed back. Another killer close by, and one not friendly, he was sure. Cat and mouse, with Cassady feeling very much the mouse. His gaze roved. Through a wide arch the shadowy outlines of a large table and several chairs were visible. Dining room, with the kitchen probably connecting beyond. In one corner a vagrant ray of light reflected off the dead face of a television screen.

Back against the wall, he sidled closer to the arch, wincing at the creak of floorboards. At the far side of the next room he discerned the balustrade of a circular stairwell. Mentally he placed Pinto at the top . . . waiting. At the entrance to the next room he ran his fingers along the wall until he located a light switch, threw it on just long enough to glimpse a phone on an old-fashioned buffet before he leaped back.

No gunfire, but he was certain Pinto was at the top of the stairwell. Jesus, the guy must have nerves like ice, wouldn't waste a shot until he had a clean one. Was Ape up there with him? Waiting till his eyes had adjusted to the darkness again, he dropped to the floor next to the wall and slithered around the corner into the next room. He turned his head slowly, his eyes following the dim row of balusters upward; at the top they served as an open parapet along the edge of a balcony. Still no movement, no sound, but he had the ungodly feeling of eyes watching him.

He looked toward the phone—he had to risk it. If the cord proved long enough, he could pull it into the next room. He inched toward it, his eyes on the dark balcony above. Without shifting his gaze, he fumbled for the instrument and raised it to his ear; the silence told him the wire had been cut.

Light flooded the room. *Pinto!* The name screaming in his mind, he twisted violently away. The mirror of the buffet behind him exploded in a shower of glass. He hit the floor rolling and scrambled to one side, aware of a burning in his shoulder. The *phut* came again and he felt a searing pain in his calf.

He brought the .38 around and spaced three shots along the balcony before he scrambled toward the doorway beyond; a third shot splintered the edge of the framing as he hurled himself through it. Breathing heavily, he twisted back. A light switch at the top of the stairs! He hadn't thought of that. How men died. But Pinto was damned cool; the three shots hadn't fazed him one bit.

Pinto was up there with no way down! He had him trapped! He felt a wave of jubilance, as quickly suppressed. Pinto above him and Ape . . . where? A goddamned pincer play, with him in the middle. Hurriedly reloading the gun, he tried to fathom Pinto's next move.

Cassady pictured him at the edge of the balcony, his weapon homed in squarely on the doorway. He looked around the shadowy room. An old stove, cupboards, a sink; the door beyond probably led to the screen porch he'd seen earlier. Ape probably had that covered.

He felt the swift rush of time, fleeting seconds that could mean life or death for Dom Perrotti. He returned his gaze to the dark dining room. Would Pinto bite on his own trick? He weighed his chances, saw no alternative—not with Pinto above him, Ape behind. He edged his hand around the doorframe, groped and found the light switch. The .38 ready, he threw the switch, thrust half his body back into the dining room. He glimpsed dark eyes that seemed enormous in a thin face before Pinto, caught by surprise, dropped to the floor. A thin hand shot out between the balusters holding a weapon; the attached silencer made it appear, to Cassady, like a cannon. His own .38 bucked as a bullet screamed past his ear, smashed into the wall behind him. The acrid smell of cordite stung his nostrils. A second bullet clipped his shoulder. The .38 held steady, he triggered it again, saw the weapon above drop from a nerveless hand, clatter against the dining room floor.

Cassady took the steps three at a time. A quick glance at Pinto's sprawled body told him he had no worry from that source. He cast a fast look below. The crash of gunfire would have put Ape on his toes; he'd be certain someone had died but he wouldn't know who. And Pretty Boy's killer . . . it perturbed him that he couldn't put that one together.

He stepped back from the edge of the balcony and looked

around—five doors, light seeping out from under the one at the far end. He crossed the balcony silently. The .38 ready, he stepped to one side, threw the door open, darted a quick look in.

For a moment he stood stock-still, his mind retreating to the scene of Skousen's death. The bloody, half-naked figure tied to a chair, the severed ears and nipples and cut throat, the angry splotches caused by burns—this was the same. In death, as in life, Bennie Worth's white lumpy body appeared grotesque, obscene.

Cassady tore his eyes away. If there was a letter, Pinto had it—his methods guaranteed that—but Bennie had been tortured long past the point when he'd talked. Pinto was worse than a goddamned animal. The mechanics of such a twisted, sadistic mind eluded him.

He retreated to the crumpled figure on the balcony and turned it face up; the glazed eyes that stared at him seemed accusatory. Pinto had died quickly, a bullet above one eye. He frisked the pockets. The letter, written on cheap stationery, was tucked into a wallet. He glanced at the room below and moved closer to the light; the childish scrawl was all but undecipherable. Cassady caught his breath at the words: . . . *and Angelo Geraci killed the cop's wife and* . . .

Cassady's head snapped up as the lights were switched off from below. He leaped backward and hit the floor. *Ape!* Thrusting the letter and wallet into his pocket, he grasped his .38. Crawling to the edge of the balcony, he peered cautiously down below between the balusters. He had the impression of shadowy movement, was trying to place a strange sloshing sound when the strong scent of gasoline struck his nostrils.

Trapped, Jesus . . .! Scuttling back from the edge, he leaped to his feet. He suppressed the impulse to run to the staircase, remembering he was in exactly the same position he'd had Pinto in.

He was casting for ways of escape when the room below

196

exploded into a leaping fireball which momentarily shot flames above the level of the balcony. Acrid smoke billowed up, attacking his eyes and nostrils. With it came a wave of heat which drove him back against the wall. Crackling sounds like that of a fusillade of a machine gun pinged in his ears. He backed into the room and slammed the door, filled with the knowledge that within minutes the entire house would be one gigantic flaming torch.

Cassady threw a quick look at Bennie's bloody body; the house would be his pyre; his own, too, if he didn't get out damned fast. He switched off the light and ran to the narrow turret window, opened it, looked at the ground some twenty feet below. He could hang from the ledge, drop. With luck he'd only break his legs.

But Ape knew—would be waiting! Jesus, while he was wriggling through the narrow window Ape could pick him off at his leisure. He suppressed his sense of urgency. Running back to the door, he opened it, recoiled from the blast of heat. Flames were leaping up with crackling, splintery sounds. The stairwell was already engulfed. His body pressed against the wall, he made his way to the adjoining room. One glance at the narrow window told him he was no better off than before. The next room would be the same.

He dashed to the last door at the far end of the balcony. The light of the flames showed a stairwell going upward. An attic! He hesitated. Unless there was a dormer window . . . he decided he had no choice.

At the top of the stairs he peered into a musty darkness. Old trunks, boxes, junk—the throwaways of decades were barely visible. A fiery glow in the periphery of his eye brought his head around; he realized it was the reflection of flames on a window. Sighting it, his heart beat faster.

He picked his way toward it, tripped and fell. He pushed himself up, wincing at sudden pains in his shoulder and calf, remembered that was where Pinto's first bullets had struck him. He reached the narrow window and looked

197

down at a steeply-pitched roof. Could he cling to that without hurtling over the edge? How far the drop? He had no choice unless he wanted to fry. He darted a look behind him—fiery tongues were shooting up through the floor boards. He groped for a latch. Finding none he smashed the glass with the butt of his .38, ran the barrel around the edges to knock off the loose shards.

The window frame was a tight fit; for a panicky moment he thought too tight. Junk behind him, exploding into flames, filled the attic with heat and smoke. Gasping for air, he finally managed to push himself through, then lay prone and tried to dig his fingers into the old shingles to keep from sliding precipitously as he edged downward.

A tongue of flame shot through the roof off to one side and the crackling roar grew louder. How much longer before the whole damned thing went? A minute? Two minutes? He felt his toes reach the edge of the roof, then cautiously turned until he could peer down. Through a swirl of smoke he saw the crown of the pepper tree some eight or ten feet below. The glow from the lower windows, dancing on the branches, gave the impression they were already in flames. Could he make it? Like dropping into hell.

Okay, quit stalling. Smiling grimly at his own advice, he clung to the shingles while lowering his body over the edge. His legs drawn up to protect himself as best he could, he gave a silent prayer and let go.

A sharp branch ripped his side, followed by a bone-crunching blow against his shins, a second dizzying blow at the side of his jaw. He had the wild sensation of pinwheeling before he came to rest, head down. Had Ape seen him? He subdued a stab of fear and fumbled for his .38, relieved to find it secure in his pocket.

Painfully freeing himself, he gripped the weapon while trying to scan the area below in the light of the dancing flames. Movement? Everything was movement . . . a world that twisted and danced and leaped in grotesque shadows thrown by the blazing house. The crackling had risen to a thunder. A window below, exploding from internal heat, sent shards of glass that slashed his face and hands.

He climbed gingerly to a lower branch, aware of a nauseous dizziness that threw his eyes out of focus; every part of him was filled with stabbing pain. Ape was either waiting or he wasn't—at the thought he dropped the last eight or ten feet, landing with a jar that all but drove his legs up into his body. He lurched to an upright position, swaying, trying to make sense of what was real and what was shadow.

Perrotti! Jesus, he had to get help for Perrotti! Another ball of flame exploded and in the periphery of its light he glimpsed a figure turned from him in profile. *Not Ape!* Trying to align the .38 he wondered how he knew. Abruptly the flames subsided and the figure was lost again.

Cassady stared into the darkness, dazed. *Not Ape!* The words came audibly and he realized he'd spoken them. There'd been a difference, something his subconscious had detected. Maybe Pretty Boy's killer . . . He swayed, remembered Perrotti. Dazed, he staggered toward the street. Dimly he became aware of a figure that seemed to grow out of the ground in front of him—short, pudgy. He automatically tabulated the data before the awareness of its meaning struck him.

Geraci! Recognition came like a physical blow. After all this . . . Geraci! He was trying to lift the .38 when a bullet from behind drove him reeling to the ground. Vaguely he thought: You blew it. The *phut-phut* of a silenced weapon echoed in his brain and almost dreamily he wondered why the bullets weren't striking him.

"*You double-crossing bastard . . .!*" The choked cry came from behind. He had the nebulous thought that Geraci was erasing the last of his tracks. Except for Sam Cassady, he told himself dully. The wail of a distant siren splintered the air.

In the dim light he had the impression of the pudgy figure drawing closer, could see Geraci's face. To make certain they both were dead? But he wasn't! He wanted to laugh wildly. Gripping the .38, he pushed himself upright to his knees.

"I'm Cassady," he said. He glimpsed the startled expression on the jowly face, heard the dull *phut-phut* of a silencer, felt the bullets slam into his body with numbing force as he triggered the .38.

Caught in blackness, he fell again.

12

His EYES OPENED TO a shadowy whiteness—a weaving, bobbing, listing whiteness without form or definition. He blinked to clear his vision while he groped with the murkiness in his mind. Crackling flames danced around him, then he was plunging down and down and down into an awesome blackness.

He shuddered and the flames vanished; everything was shadows and out of them walked a pudgy figure. *Geraci! The phut-phut of a silenced gun*—everything swarmed back with a rush. The shot from behind, the pudgy figure ahead, bullets slamming into him as he triggered the .38.

A rustling sound reached him and a woman clad in white came into view. A nurse, he thought dimly. Cool hands touched his arms, he felt a stinging, then he slept. A dreamless sleep.

When he awoke again, a nurse—the same one?—was bustling around his bed. "Ah, you're awake." Gray eyes in a round, pleasant face.

"How . . . how long?" He struggled to clear his mind.

"Two days. How do you feel?" The voice was soft, warm.

"Good." Cassady had a vision of the startled expression in the pudgy face as he triggered the .38. "Great," he added.

The pleasant face smiled. "An exaggeration, I'm sure."

"Have . . . have I had any visitors?" A sense of urgency gripped him. "Cindy . . . Mrs. O'Neal?"

"Every day, but you're not allowed visitors yet."

"How soon?"

"Perhaps another day or two. That'll be up to the doctor."

"Perrotti . . . Dom Perrotti? Do you know?"

"He's doing fine. He's in the next room. Now you'd better rest." She took his temperature, had him swallow a pill, then withdrew. Sleep came again.

His vision cleared and Garmont's angular, long-jawed face swam into view. Hooded eyes were watching him. "How do you feel, Sam?"

"Great." He blinked to clear his vision. "How's Dom?"

"It was touch and go for a while but he'll make it. We haven't been able to talk with him yet."

"That bad?"

"Bad enough, but Dom's tough. How did he get into the act?"

"How?" Cassady stalled, groping for an answer, knew that Garmont knew he was stalling. Perrotti had been working on his own; the question told him that. But why? He looked back at Garmont's waiting eyes. "He must have spotted me, tailed me . . . hoped I'd lead him to Bennie. When he saw what was happening, he tried to save my ass."

"That's about the way we put it together, Sam."

"Geraci?"

"You got him dead center."

"The letter . . . I have a letter."

"We have it, Sam. Not that it means much—a dead man's charge that he knew Geraci and Skousen were involved in Nancy's murder. But that's academic, isn't it?"

202

"Yeah, it's over." He thought of Cindy, their future.

"Most of it looks pretty clear-cut. . . ." He brought back his attention, visualizing the scenes as Garmont spoke. Geraci had shot him, had killed Mark Kopke; ballistics proved that. A short length of pipe and a switchblade knife found on Kopke's body had almost certainly been the weapons used to kill August Miller and Leo Hein. Too, Hein's body had reeked of gasoline. Cassady realized that Hein must have been the man he'd tagged as Ape. " . . . six dead have been recovered from the ashes," Garmont said.

"Six?" Cassady was startled. "I saw Pinto, Bennie, two women."

"Another male and female had been killed in another room," he explained. "In case you didn't know, the place was a whorehouse . . . Mae Hammond's. Vice filled us in on that."

"Kopke . . . who was he?"

"A two-bit killer."

"I don't get it. Why did he kill Miller and Hein?" The thought he'd had earlier came to the fore. "Or was he working for Geraci, trying to cover Geraci's tracks?"

"That's the way we see it, Sam, but he wasn't smart enough to know how those things work."

"The goddamned Syndicate!"

Garmont shook his head. "It looks like Geraci worked this one on his own."

"You know better than that, Marcos." Cassady's anger flared.

"Reason it out, Sam. That outfit has billions and billions at stake now. Do you think the top man in this area would risk something like this? And if he did, do you think he'd pull off this kind of a sloppy job? When it comes to that, we can't even prove a tie between Geraci and the Syndicate. Remember what I said about corporation presidents and board chairmen? That's where the deep shadows lie."

"How about Kopke? He's no damned board chairman."

"He was on Orkie's payroll, a trucker over at the firm on

Alameda. Not that he ever drove a truck, but that part of the business is legitimate. It's the same with the rest of them—no proof. But you know the truth about Geraci and your man is dead. Be satisfied, Sam."

"Yeah, judge, jury and hangman."

"That's understandable."

"That bastard would have walked away free and clear, Marcos."

"Yes, he would have." Garmont rose. "You did a good job, Sam. Later you can brace yourself for a mountain of paperwork."

Perrotti appeared asleep when Cassady edged into the room. The knife-slash across his cheek appeared a livid purple against the sallow flesh of his face. Cassady was appalled at how thin he looked.

He was starting to withdraw when Perrotti opened his eyes. "Sam . . ." He gestured weakly toward a chair.

"Just checking to make sure you're not malingering," Cassady said. He sat by the bed, wincing from the pain in his side, where a branch had torn the flesh away from his ribs.

"More likely the other way around," Perrotti observed. "You look fit for duty."

"Yeah, back to the old highways." Cassady felt a pleasure at the thought of getting back behind the wheel of the old black-and-white cruiser. "I came to thank you, Dom. You were a damned fool, but thank you."

"For what? Barging in like a damned rookie and getting shot?"

"For warning me about Pinto, for one thing. I didn't know he was on my ass," he lied.

"He was loose too long, Sam."

"And you just happened to show up when I walked into a hornet's nest, right?"

"I was tailing Pinto," Perrotti admitted.

Cassady grinned. "Watching you drive the other night, I thought about recruiting you for the Traffic Division. Interested?"

"That scared hell out of me." Perrotti smiled. "Tell me, do you always make U-turns like that?"

"Only when I'm trying to shake off a tail. Incidentally, Garmont will probably be in to see you before long."

"I expect he will."

"I told him how you got into the mess." Cassady related his conversation with the inspector. "Aside from who you were tailing, that was about it, wasn't it?"

"Just about." Perrotti brought out a brown envelope from under the covers and gazed pensively at it.

"Fan mail?"

"Photos and negatives from an incident in my earlier years," Perrotti explained. "An old man sent them, knew I'd like to have them."

"Good, you can add them to your scrapbook."

Perrotti shook his head. "A scrapbook I don't need, Sam. Rip 'em up, flush them down the john, will you?"

"Yeah, scrapbooks can get messy." He glanced at the envelope, knowing he didn't want to see its contents. Ripping it into small squares, he went to the bathroom and flushed them down the toilet.

When he came back, Perrotti said, "To echo the old saw, I feel born again."

"Me, too." Cassady grinned. "How would you like to be a best man?"